John Creasey – Master Storyteller

Born in Surrey, England in 1908 into a poor family in which there were nine children, John Creasey grew up to be a true master story teller and international sensation. His more than 600 crime, mystery and thriller titles have now sold 80 million copies in 25 languages. These include many popular series such as *Gideon of Scotland Yard*, *The Toff*, *Dr Palfrey* and *The Baron*.

Creasy wrote under many pseudonyms, explaining that booksellers had complained he totally dominated the 'C' section in stores. They included:

> *Gordon Ashe, M E Cooke, Norman Deane, Robert Caine Frazer, Patrick Gill, Michael Halliday, Charles Hogarth, Brian Hope, Colin Hughes, Kyle Hunt, Abel Mann, Peter Manton, J J Marric, Richard Martin, Rodney Mattheson, Anthony Morton* and *Jeremy York*.

Never one to sit still, Creasey had a strong social conscience, and stood for Parliament several times, along with founding the One Party Alliance which promoted the idea of government by a coalition of the best minds from across the political spectrum.

He also founded the British Crime Writers' Association, which to this day celebrates outstanding crime writing. The Mystery Writers of America bestowed upon him the Edgar Award for best novel and then in 1969 the ultimate Grand Master Award. John Creasey's stories are as compelling today as ever.

D1732806

THE BARON SERIES

Blood Red

(Red Eye for the Baron)

John Creasey

HOUSE OF
STRATUS

Chapter One

Queer Customer

One had to enter Quinns to believe such a shop still existed.

It was almost heresy to call it a 'shop'. The senior and the junior members of the staff called it 'an establishment', and others described it as a gallery. It was narrow and deep, and had stood for three hundred years and more in the heart of fashionable London, serving the same kind of customers, clients, or patrons, according to one's choice of word.

Whatever one called it, it was a home of beautiful things, most of them very old, *objets d'art* of incredible rarity or extraordinary beauty. From China and Japan, from India and Ceylon, from the land of the Pharaohs and from Rome, from the darkness of Africa of a hundred years ago, from the glory of Italy in the days of Michelangelo to the savage beauty of the early days of Tsarist Russia, these precious things were cherished here for a while, and then passed on.

Often they were passed on with regret and even sadness, for all who served at Quinns loved what they sold. A vase, a carving, a painting, a piece of hand-wrought silver, a golden medallion of an almost-forgotten age – all of these would be handled reverently.

Only the present owner of Quinns, John Mannering, laughed at this solemnity, but it was a gentle, understanding laughter. He bought and sold *objets* which varied in value from a few to many thousands of pounds, and yet did not take himself or Quinns anything like as seriously as the staff took both. But it was good that the staff should do so, for they so impressed the customers, clients, and patrons.

The visitors to Quinns were mostly people who collected coins or jade, jewels or amber, miniatures or silver, pictures or antique furniture – these and a thousand other things. Most of them loved what they collected. It was fitting that they should enter this old, graceful shop, where the soft lighting came from many lamps, each placed so that it showed some particular *objet* to advantage. It was rather like entering a cathedral.

It was also fitting that the older members of the staff should be like priests and the younger ones like acolytes.

It was as well that John Mannering could chuckle about all this, once the door of his office was closed, or when he was at home with his wife in their studio flat in Chelsea, not very far from the Thames.

One of the attractions for Mannering was the variety and the uncertainty of life at Quinns. One never knew what was going to be brought in next, or who would bring it. The only certain thing was that each week, if not each day, would bring some oddity.

The day which brought Theodorus Wray was the red letter day of the year.

It was a bright morning in May, and the chill had crept into Quinns, where repairs were being carried out on the antiquated central heating system. Larraby, the shop manager, silvery haired and frail-looking, and Sylvester, the senior assistant, bald headed and plump, were rubbing their pale hands together and trying not to complain aloud, for the three younger members of the staff were bearing the chill with commendable fortitude. It was a little after ten o'clock. John Mannering was in his office, and the door was closed, a sign to the staff that he must not be disturbed.

They knew that he was studying a collection of emeralds, offered for sale by a little-known dealer.

The outside world passed Quinns by. The shop was in a narrow street, with only a few exclusive establishments, and at the far end was an open space, cleared years ago by bombing. When people walked, they walked quietly, and when they drove, they drove cautiously, because of the narrowness of the road. It should have been a one-way street, of course, but was not. So everyone took a little extra care, and the passing of cars was almost as stately as the passing of broughams and hansom cabs had been a few generations ago.

Every member of the staff was concentrating on his job: polishing, cataloguing, valuing, or simply moving certain things, and all was still and silent outside until, out of this hush, there came a squeal of tyres. Every head jerked up. In every mind was the thought: 'smash-and-grab.' Larraby's hand moved, almost a reflex action, towards the telephone. A car shot into view.

The first thought of each one who saw this was that the car was passing by, because it streaked into their vision, then suddenly seemed to gather itself up, tyres still squealing, until it stopped with its driver's door exactly opposite the front door of Quinns.

The driver was alone.

Larraby's hand lingered only lightly on the telephone, for smash-and-grab raiders seldom came singly. For that matter, they seldom came at all, but they had been known; and sneak thieves came often, so that there was a kind of alarm drill among the staff. No word was needed, but Thomas, the largest and strongest of the junior members, went towards the door, while the others lined themselves up, not too obviously, so that a dubious or suspect stranger would have to pass each one. It was a kind of defence in depth.

The driver was a youthful-looking man.

The car was a scarlet and green Cadillac, shiny and very new.

For a moment the driver sat staring at the shop door, and Larraby's fingers tightened their grip, for he was aware that all kinds of methods were used in raids on shops like Quinns, and this might be a way of disarming them all.

Then Larraby's fingers positively clutched the telephone, for the driver moved. The opening of the car door, the stepping out, the closing of the door – all seemed to be done in a single, lightning-like movement. A man of medium height, hatless, fair-haired, immaculately dressed in pale brown, stepped to the window.

Thomas was within a few feet of the door, a dark-haired, powerful young man of twenty-seven.

The driver of the Cadillac studied the window.

This was a small one, seldom containing more than a single piece. The toughened glass was almost unbreakable. Today, the window was dressed in rich dark blue velvet, and on this reposed a single diamond ring of such beauty and such value that sight and even thought of it made some people gasp for breath. In the centre diamond there was a hint of colour, of pink; the credulous believed that this was indeed the blood of the first owner of the ring, a queen of Babylon remembered only because its glowing beauty had been hers.

There was a magnificent story which had become a legend: that the queen had been cold and arrogant, repulsing everyone by her indifference, and beloved by none, until she possessed the ring. From that day on, man had only to look at her to love and desire, and even to possess.

The fair-haired driver studied the ring much as a schoolboy might study a football, tennis racquet, or bat. He stood there for a long time – time enough for the staff to see that he was not so young as he looked – in the middle forties, perhaps. Suddenly he seemed electrified into movement, reached the door, thrust it open, and stepped inside. He arrived so quickly that Thomas had no chance to open the door, and hardly time to say, 'Good morning, sir,' before the visitor said briskly, 'How much is that ring in the window?'

Thomas gulped.

A kind of shiver seemed to run through the others, having least effect on Larraby, who took his hand from the telephone but did not move away. The question was almost a form of heresy. There had been no time for reflection, no time for contemplation, no time to absorb the atmosphere, and for that matter no time to realise that such a jewel should be spoken of in a hushed and reverent voice.

'Er—' Thomas began.

'Where's the manager?' demanded the man, still in that brisk, clipped way. He now proved to have very light blue eyes, and to have a certain rugged handsomeness. His movements were beautifully controlled. Impatience showed in his eyes when he walked past Thomas to the next youthful assistant. 'You heard me. Where's the boss?'

Larraby came forward as Thomas shepherded the visitor, and said, 'All right, Thomas. Richard, I will see if I can help this gentleman.' Massive Thomas and medium-sized Richard withdrew, leaving snowy-haired Larraby and Sylvester, and the youngest and smallest of the assistants, between the newcomer and Mannering's office. 'Now, sir, if you will be good enough to tell me what you require, I will be glad to help.'

'Are you John Mannering?'

'No, sir, Mr Mannering is—'

'He in?'

'I will find out, sir, if you will—'

'He's either in or he isn't; someone ought to know,' said the caller, whose fair hair showed, at close quarters, some signs of hidden grey. He slipped past Larraby so that he was confronted with the smallest assistant, who was not yet eighteen, and nervous even at the best of times. This lad had a little baby face and curly brown hair. The stranger stopped, put his head on one side, and quite unexpectedly grinned. 'You Mannering?'

'N—n—no, sir!'

'All right, Henry,' Larraby said, and in turn pushed past the fair-haired stranger. 'Now, sir, I will gladly—'

'What did you call him?' demanded the stranger. 'Mr Mannering?'

'No, not Mannering, what did you call him?' The caller stabbed a forefinger towards the junior assistant's chest, and Henry seemed ready to collapse.

Larraby was equal to this as to all occasions. 'I called him by his Christian name, sir. This is a custom among the junior staff. The name is Henry.'

'Don't say it,' protested the stranger, and again he flashed that swift, vivid grin. 'The muscle man is Thomas, the middle man is Richard, and this is Henry. That right?'

'That is right, sir.' Even Larraby began to perspire.

'Tom, Dick, and Harry! You pick the staff?'

'Subject to Mr Mannering's approval, sir, yes, but I do assure you that the choice of names was quite fortuitous.'

'For—too—it—tuss, eh,' echoed the stranger. His eyes seemed to become even more pale as he narrowed them to peer at Larraby. He was silent for a moment; it was like a lull in a storm. Then he rapped, as lightning, 'How much does he pay you?'

'I beg your pardon, sir?'

'You heard me,' the newcomer said. 'What's the matter with you folks around here; haven't you ever heard plain English? How much?'

'I really—' Larraby actually stumbled over the words, and the strain was so great that no one even smiled.

No one had noticed that the door of the office was open a few inches, and John Mannering was standing at it, just able to see the customer, and able to hear every word.

'Whatever you're paid, I'll double it,' the man offered crisply. 'You've got yourself a big raise. Just stay the way you are; I don't want you any different. What do they call that tie you're wearing – let me see, I've heard— Got it! It's a cravat. Okay, you'll always wear a cravat. How about starting right away?'

Larraby clutched desperately at his self-control. It took a great deal of clutching, and he was not able to reply immediately. Sylvester was by his side, and Henry had backed deep into the shop, as if to keep himself safely out of the clutches of this maniac.

'Okay, so you've got to give notice,' the visitor conceded. 'Instead of notice, give money. I'll fix Mannering; how about fetching Mannering now? I haven't got all day to waste; I just want to buy that ring and take it away with me. You join my staff when you can.'

He glanced round, saw the opening door, and then saw Mannering. The staff also saw the owner, who was smiling, as if genuinely amused. He was very handsome, especially when smiling. He was several inches taller than the stranger, who spun round and approached him, asking with clipped brusqueness, 'Are you John Mannering?'

Chapter Two

Deal

'Yes,' said Mannering. 'Good morning.'

For the first time since he had entered the shop, the man seemed to hesitate, as if not quite sure what to say. Probably this was due to Mannering's smile, and the amusement in his eyes. It did not last long. The caller thrust his right hand forward, and announced as if he were known by name the whole world over, 'I'm Theodorus Wray.'

Mannering had never heard the name Theodorus, and never heard of this man, but he allowed his hand to be taken. The grip from lean, cool fingers was quick and firm.

'Don't know how much you heard,' he said. 'I've come for the ring in the window. How much is it?'

'Didn't you come for my manager, too?' asked Mannering.

Wray glanced round at Larraby.

'Is he your manager? He's in the wrong job, Mr Mannering; he can't tell me how much that ring costs! Don't tell me you fix the price according to the customer's bankroll. I was assured that you didn't work that way.'

Mannering chuckled, and, chuckling, gave Larraby the straw he had been wanting. A little faintly, but with a glimmer of a smile at his lips, Larraby said, 'I did not commit myself to entering Mr Wray's employ, sir.'

'The manager of a place like this must get quite a packet,' Wray said, almost musingly, 'but my offer stands. Whatever salary you get, I'll double it.'

'And you can't say fairer than that,' declared Mannering.

'You've said it. Now, let's get down to business, Mr Mannering. How about the ring? What's the price?'

Everyone in the shop watched Mannering, three of them with bated breath. Each knew that the approximate value of the ring was a little over forty thousand pounds; and each knew that some rich men would give twice that sum to place it in their collections. They would guard it with massive locks, steel bars, and armed men, and show it to a marvelling world once or twice a year through glass which a pile driver could not break.

Theodorus Wray thrust his arms upward, both hands clenched, and his voice rose an octave.

'What's going on around here? I want to buy the ring for my girl friend. I want her to have the best engagement ring that money can buy. I've got the money, I've got the girl, all I want to know is the price. How about some action, Mr Mannering? Now, give.'

Thomas, Richard, and Henry gasped.

Sylvester put a hand to his forehead and breathed something that sounded like, 'Oh, no.'

Larraby, taking his cue from Mannering, smiled amiably. Mannering chuckled infectiously, partly because of the effect of all this on the staff, partly because of the expression in Theodorus Wray's eyes. He had seen the same kind of look in the eyes of a tourist in France when the waiter did not understand his French. In a moment, exasperation would turn to annoyance and perhaps to anger.

'Now what the heck—' began Wray, sharply.

'To a collector, that ring is worth about a hundred thousand pounds,' Mannering said, keeping a straight face. 'Intrinsically, the diamonds are worth perhaps forty thousand pounds. You may not approve of the distinction in values, but there it is.'

'I don't want it on the cheap. I'll give you seventy-five thousand pounds for it,' the man declared briskly.

That brusque got past even Mannering's guard. It turned the rest of the staff into human stalagmites. It made everyone oblivious of the fact that there was a street outside and people passing to and fro, some even standing and admiring the red and green Cadillac, and one girl peering in at the shop window. She was looking towards the men and the far end of the shop, not at the diamond on the soft velvet.

'You could hold it for a collector who'll pay more,' Wray said, briskly, 'but how many are there with that kind of money? They'll haggle, anyway. And you can't fool me with all this museum atmosphere; you're in business for what you can get out of it. I've made some inquiries about you. Seventy-five thousand pounds for the Red Eye of Love is a competitive price, and if you were offered it from a collector this week, you'd take it. And you'd make yourself a tidy pile too. I know more or less how much you paid for it. So how about a deal? I want that Red Eye, and that's weakening my position in bargaining, but I get good advice and I'm advised that you trade on the level. Is it a deal?'

He was in absolute earnest.

'God bless my soul!' exclaimed Sylvester, and sat down heavily on an oak chair which had been carved as a labour of love four hundred years ago.

'If it's the money you're worried about, come round to my bank,' invited Theodorus Wray.

'It isn't the money,' said Mannering, and felt the need to take this Theodorus much more seriously than he had. 'There are certain other factors which have to be taken into account.'

'You had an offer?' Wray barked.

'No, not yet, but—'

The shop door opened.

It was positively unique that it should open without anyone noticing the light which glowed in several places, warning the staff that somebody else was coming in. The light system was another precaution against theft. But no one had seen a light or heard a sound, and the first indication of the opening door was a firm, feminine voice.

'Theo, you're not to do it.'

Everyone started, and turned or stared towards the door. There stood a girl, quite young, neat, probably nice-looking, although her back was towards the window, and her face and figure in shadow. She was slim, though, and not very tall. The door closed of its own volition, and she came forward, making no sound at all on the strip of carpet between the door and Mannering's office.

'Hi, honey!' Wray greeted, and waved to her; then burst out laughing. 'Mind you don't fall over Tom, Dick, and Harry!' By then, Thomas and Richard were making way for the girl, and Henry was almost out of sight and certainly out of her way. 'I want you to meet the most beautiful girl in the world,' Wray went on. 'Nothing's too good for my fiancée.' He studied Mannering's face, as if wanting to make sure that he was properly impressed.

Mannering was.

As the girl drew nearer and he could see her clearly, he realised that there were many who would agree with Theodorus Wray about her beauty. But it wasn't ethereal, and it wasn't the picture postcard kind. This was the beauty one might find unexpectedly in a crofter's cottage in the Highlands, or a farm on the Sussex Downs: it was a natural quality, which make-up helped a little but certainly didn't create. She moved beautifully too. She was dark but not raven-haired; her complexion was more fair than dark, her eyes gave the impression that she could laugh easily.

'Honey, this is John Mannering, the guy with quite a reputation. You want to know what I found out about him? His pedigree's full of blue blood, if you're interested. He's worth plenty; he's said to know more about lumps of ice and strings of pearls than anyone in England; he's an expert antiquarian – but that's not the best bit. He ... '

The girl was looking at Mannering with an expression which seemed to say helplessly, 'I'm sorry, but there's no way of stopping him.'

'... is the most famous private eye in England. What do you know about that? You should see what the newspapers say about him. I've looked up some old files, and are they pleased with the great John

Mannering! Quote. "Consulted by Scotland Yard on all matters concerned with *objets d'art* and precious stones." End quote. And his wife—'

'We'll leave my wife out of this,' Mannering said, through another chuckle. 'Would you mind telling me the name of the most beautiful girl in the world?'

Wray's eyes lit up.

'You agree about that?'

'I most certainly do.'

'You know, honey, I like this guy,' said Theodorus Wray. 'Never mind his reputation, I like him.' He took the girl's left hand and squeezed it, touched the engagement finger with his lips, and went on, 'Sure, she's got a name. Rosamund. With a U. Can you beat it? Rosamund Morrel, M–O double–R–E–one L. Honey, I've got a hunch that it's going to be a perfect fit.' He looked up at Mannering. 'How about fetching that ring and trying it on?'

'Josh, will you fetch the ring?' asked Mannering.

'Theo, I don't intend to try it on, and I'm not going to let you make a fool of yourself,' Rosamund Morrel declared, but she did not withdraw her hand. 'There are thousands of engagement rings that will show everyone what a rich man you are; you needn't try to prove that you're the richest man in the world.'

'I never said I was,' denied Theodorus Wray. 'Some of the others guys are pretty cagey about how much they've got. I consider I'm in the first dozen, that's all.' He was still completely in earnest. 'There's just one engagement ring for you, honey. When I read about it in the *Collector and Connoisseur* last night, I got busy. First I checked on Mannering and this shop, and they stood up, then I checked on the Red Eye of Love, and that stood up. So here I am, with a firm offer, and I've a feeling that Mannering isn't going to turn it down. If it's too big or too small,' he added anxiously, 'can it be altered to fit?'

'It can be adjusted,' Mannering assured him solemnly. 'Quickly.'

Larraby was already at the window.

'It's a complete waste of time,' Rosamund insisted. 'I refuse even to try it on.'

'How about that?' Wray appealed to Mannering, with a broad smile. 'Most girls would be wondering what they could make me buy next, but not my Rosamund; she tries to save me money. She doesn't realise that I don't have to save. I couldn't spend all I've got if I lived to be a thousand years, which I won't.' He saw Larraby approaching with the ring on a small velvet pad, opened his mouth to go on, but stopped.

The beauty and the glory of the ring silenced him.

Larraby bore it on both hands, as if it were an offering. Although the light was not good, it seemed to take fire near the ring itself. Near Mannering was another lamp, and its light fell upon the ring and made the fires burn with unutterable beauty. It was as if the ring were a living, breathing creature.

From the centre diamond there stabbed scintillas of flame-red.

The girl stood as if overwhelmed. Mannering, who had heard of this ring's fame for many years, and had always longed to see it, felt as he so often did: that life was rewarding if one could gaze upon such splendour even once. Theodorus Wray tightened his lips as the ring came nearer, and the red of the centre stone seemed to reflect in his pale blue eyes.

He broke the silence, huskily. 'Gee,' he said, 'that's a honey.'

"Theo, I tell you—' Rosamund's voice broke. 'Oh, it's unthinkable. Please take it away, Mr Mannering.'

'You don't seem to understand, honey, that's for you,' said Wray. His voice was still a little husky, as he looked from the diamond to her eyes. They were grey and very clear, and just now touched with a kind of anguish, as if the temptation to accept this priceless gift was fighting with her knowledge that it was not only absurd but a kind of sacrilege.

'Okay for me to handle it?' Wray asked Mannering, and Mannering nodded. He was aware of the tension in Larraby, could imagine that his manager was thinking that this might be a trick, after all, that some sleight of hand would make the ring vanish; or else, at this very moment, that accomplices would storm into the shop.

Wray picked up the ring slowly. Obviously he was surprised to find how heavily it weighed. He hesitated; then, with his free hand, took Rosamund's.

She tried to snatch herself free.

He held her so that she couldn't, and moved the ring closer to her fingers. The beauty seemed to make her powerless, as if mesmerised. Very slowly and reverently Wray placed it on her engagement finger. Then he kissed the finger.

Mannering saw the girl's eyes film with tears; Wray's eyes were soft, and his smile gentle. 'Okay, honey?' His voice was soft as well.

'It—it's madness.' She could hardly bring the words out, and was still mesmerised by the stone; and now those red scintillas flashed red into her eyes, like subdued fire.

'I've got the money and you've got the ring,' Wray declared. 'How about my offer, Mannering? This is just about the first thing in my life I've allowed a man to know how badly I want a thing. You've only got to state your price.'

'My price is seventy-five thousand pounds,' Mannering responded, just as quietly.

There was silence.

Then the girl snatched her hand away, pulled at the ring so that it came off, and thrust it blindly towards Mannering, crying, 'No, I can't! Take it back. I won't have it, I don't want it! Theo, you must be mad!'

She turned and rushed towards the door and the street.

She ran out.

The ring was in Mannering's hand.

Theodorus Wray was smiling that gentle smile again. 'Well, what about that?' he inquired proudly. 'There's integrity for you. Integrity is the rarest quality I know anywhere in the world. You'd agree about that, Mannering. Now, I want to settle the deal and I want to have that ring just as soon as I can. Rosamund will see it my way with a little persuasion. You want to know something? That girl didn't know I was worth a penny when we met, or when she promised to marry me. No, sir, she didn't know a thing. We met by accident, and the moment I saw her I told myself that she was mine for keeps. Yes, sir. And now she is mine for keeps, so the Red Eye of Love is hers for keeps. How long will it take to fix it? I anticipated you would want a surety, so I arranged that with my bank.'

'Before you go any further,' Mannering demurred, 'are you positive you're right? That ring is worth a fortune. Your fiancée is justifiably terrified of it. She couldn't wear it, except on special occasions, and—'

'Why not?' Wray was suddenly aggressive.

'Surely it's obvious. She would be in danger all the time; you'd have to have protection.'

'I'm all the protection Rosamund and the ring need,' said Wray crisply. 'Haven't you ever heard of such a thing as insurance? Let me tell you something, Mannering. I don't hold with collecting precious things like this and shutting them up and permitting a few people to take a peek at them occasionally. No, sir. Jewels weren't meant to be in a museum or a vault; they were meant to be on a woman's body. Don't tell me you disagree. Didn't you see the way that ring changed when it was on Rosamund's finger? Why, it glowed so red that it came alive! That's one ring which isn't going to be hidden away from the world. She's going to wear it. And maybe a lot of other people will start wearing their jewels, too. The younger they are, the better; you don't expect diamonds to come to life on an old woman with one foot in the grave, do you?' He stopped, challengingly.

'No,' Mannering agreed, very deliberately. He did not add that he had never heard a man express greater love for precious stones, although probably Wray did not yet realise that he loved them. 'Mr Wray, if you want to buy the ring, you can. I'd rather you thought it over and talked it over with Miss Morrel before you finally make up your mind. Shall we leave it for twenty-four hours? Then I can check your credentials, anyhow.'

'Okay,' Wray said abruptly. 'Sleeping on it won't make any difference. I'll be here for it at ten o'clock tomorrow morning. Here's a letter from Hemming and Hemming, saying I'm good for unlimited credit, and here's another letter from the All State Bank of Australia, saying the same thing, and if you want it, the Australian Minister to London knows me, and he'll vouch for me.'

He was thrusting folded documents into Mannering's hand.

'That'll be enough,' said Mannering, almost weakly. 'Thanks.'

'Thank you.' Wray nodded, and turned on his heel – and startled everyone but Mannering by the speed of his movements. 'Okay, John,' he said, and the name seemed to rocket back at Mannering as he reached the door. 'Hi, Tom, hi Dick, hi Harry!'

He went out, shot into the car, and the engine seemed to start and the wheels to turn in the same moment, and it was hard to believe that it was an illusion.

Larraby, Sylvester, and Tom, Dick, and Harry, let out their breath as the car disappeared, in a pent sigh.

Mannering's hands closed round the ring.

'Put something else in the window, Josh,' he said to Larraby. 'I'll look after this.'

Larraby said in a shaken voice, 'I'm almost persuaded of the gentleman's integrity, sir, but is it possible that the girl did know—' He left the question in mid-air.

'I'm going to do a little checking,' Mannering declared, and turned back into his office.

Before he closed the door, he heard an urgent, 'Can you spare a moment, sir?' and turned to find massive Thomas hurrying forward.

'Yes, Tom. What's on your mind?'

'I—er—I was nearer the window than anyone else, as you know, sir,' said Thomas, 'and I happened to notice a man on a motor-cycle draw up just behind the Caddy – the American car, sir. He followed again just now. As Mr Wray appears to be such a wealthy person, and as he visited here, it is conceivable that—'

'He was being followed to be robbed, or being followed by a bodyguard,' said Mannering quickly. 'Is your Vespa parked in the usual place?'

'Yes, sir!'

'Nip out and try to see where they go,' said Mannering. 'They'll have to turn round in the car park; you've half a chance.'

'Right, sir!' Thomas proved that bulk did not prevent him from being quick, and he hurried; but his movement was a crawl compared with Theodorus Wray's. Yet when the monster Cadillac slid past the window and a man on a red motorcycle followed, Thomas followed in turn, huge upon the seat of a pale blue Vespa.

'Let's wish him luck,' Mannering said, and turned at last into his office.

The Red Eye of Love lay on his desk, only half alive. Wray was quite right: a woman's body was needed to give real life to this jewel of such beauty.

Chapter Three

Rosamund Says No Again

Rosamund Morrel opened the front door of the house in Kensington where she had a two-room flat, and stepped inside. Then she turned round and looked along the street, as if expecting to see the monstrous car swing round the corner and come hurtling towards her. A little three-wheeler came trundling, instead. She closed the door and walked briskly up the narrow stairs. There were three floors and three flats; hers was at the top. An old brown hair carpet, threadbare in places, covered the stairs, and there was a strip at each landing.

Rosamund reached her own front door, hesitated, then inserted the key and opened it.

'I'll bet he'll be here in the next ten minutes,' she said in a tone of resignation, and gave an odd little laugh as she added, 'Bless him!' She took off her hat and put it on the arm of an easy chair. This was the living room; beyond was the bedroom, with a tiny cubicle in between known as the kitchen. The bathroom led off the bedroom. The house was old, the ceilings high, and the decoration could have been much less attractive. In this room, for instance, there was a pale grey paper with a tiny red motif. For furnished rooms the furniture wasn't at all bad, either. She finished ruffling her hair, and went to the window. This overlooked a small back garden, and between houses beyond she could see the High Street.

Cars and buses passed swiftly by.

She might catch a glimpse of the red and green Cadillac.

'Oh, you fool,' she said, quite loudly. 'What is there about him?'

The door leading from the cubicle and the bedroom opened, and as she spun round, in fierce alarm, Theodorus Wray said mildly, 'He's just a nice guy, I guess.'

'Theo, you fool! You made me jump so much that my heart's pounding now.'

That's just because I'm near.'

'How did you get in?'

'I stole your spare key last night.'

'Don't you realise that if the neighbours saw you, they'd—'

'I know no neighbours, see no neighbours, hear no neighbours,' declared Theo. He reached her, took her in his arms, and hugged her, making her hold her head back so that she could not avoid looking at him. It was as if he knew that her heart was thumping with excitement because of him, as if he knew that there wasn't a thing that she could deny him.

Except perhaps make her take that fantastic ring.

'Honey,' he said chidingly, 'you shouldn't have done that in front of Tom, Dick, and Harry. They're good guys. They're a bit strait-laced, but who wouldn't be, living among all those relicts?'

'You don't know what a relict is. You mean relic'

'You're too smart for me, honey!' He kissed her gently; he could be remarkably gentle. 'That Mannering's quite a guy.'

'If you say "guy" again, I'll scream!' Rosamund was only half laughing as she eased herself out of his arms and stepped back. 'And if you think you're going to make me change my mind, you're absolutely wrong.'

'That John Mannering,' said Theo, in a plummy, pseudo-Oxford voice. 'He's quite a fellah, eh, what? What a wallah, what ho?' He didn't smile, except with his eyes. 'You know what he did, hon? He sent Tom to follow Charley. He's a wise G man all right. You should have heard what the editor of the *Daily Globe* said about him. I like that chappie.' He grinned at her, showing his fine white teeth.

'I don't care what you say, I'm not going to have that ring.'

'Honey, how you do keep on! Have I said anything about a ring since I stepped in here?'

'Theo, be serious for a minute,' Rosamund pleaded. 'You must understand that I am not going to accept an engagement ring worth so much money, and I wouldn't wear it if I accepted it, and you wouldn't want that.'

'No, I guess I wouldn't,' he agreed, with a mock frown. 'Say, how about this: we'll turn it into a family heirloom. I guess it would be the very first I ever had. Didn't you like it, honey?'

'Like it? It would be like having one of the Crown Jewels!'

'That's right,' said Theo earnestly. 'That's exactly right. Fit for a queen. How did you like my gentleman friend Mannering, eh? You're mighty cagey about him.'

'I hardly noticed him.'

'That I don't believe. He's Ronald Colman, Rex Harrison, and Greg Peck rolled into one!'

Rosamund found herself laughing. She so often found herself laughing with Theo. The way he grinned with one side of his mouth, and the way he screwed up one eye in pretended disgust, the way he said the unexpected, the outrageous statement he would make – all encouraged her to laugh. To take him seriously all the time would be impossible. In some ways he was much younger than men of her own age; it was hard to realise that he was forty-four.

'Theo,' she said, 'I don't want you to misunderstand me. I think it's a wonderful thing to suggest, it's absolutely superb, but it isn't practical. You just have to learn to handle your money differently from that. It's no use buying famous diamond rings as if they were rhinestones.'

'Honey, didn't you promise to marry me?'

'Yes, I suppose I did, but—'

'You suppose you did?' He moved with one of those lightning-like surges, took her up in his arms and held her very close, and said deep in his throat, 'You promised to marry me, and don't you forget it. I can't wait until I've got the ring on your finger, and you on a honeymoon.' He kissed her until she gasped for breath, when he drew his lips away, but he didn't let her go. 'You're going to marry me, and I'll kill any guy who tries to stop us.'

He sounded almost as if he meant it.

She stared at him in alarm, seeing the grimness of his expression, which had so swiftly followed gentleness, and she was a little frightened. He meant it when he said it. He was subject to such swift changes and moments of fierce, almost ferocious temper, and she had experienced that several times in the two weeks since they had met. He lived on his nerves, and did ten men's work, but she believed that there was some other cause of these outbursts.

Was he frightened? Was it fear that tore at his nerves, making him live so tensely that some quite small thing might bring on a rage?

She knew only what he had told her about himself.

That he was English, had emigrated as a youth to Australia, made a fortune there, then gone to the United States, and literally struck oil.

'Yes, sir, ma'am,' he would say in that sometimes ludicrous attempt to speak as an American from the Deep South, 'I'm in oil, sho' thing I'm in oil, there ain't no man alive in mo' oil than I'm in.'

They had met at a cocktail party. She wasn't sure who had introduced them – possibly someone who modelled at the same photographer's studio. She had noticed him; everyone had. He'd talked outrageously even among a crowd. Then he'd espied her, and something seemed to happen to him. He had walked straight across the room, taking another man by the arm as he came, and when he reached her had said, 'Introduce us, friend.'

They had been introduced.

'Rosamund sounds just about right to me,' Theodorus had said, and added the only comment he had ever made about his childhood or his parents. 'My dad invented the name, he had some kind of an idea that it was in the Bible, so I'm Theodorus. Where are we going to have dinner tonight?'

Just like that.

She had not dined with him that night or the following night. Since then, she hadn't had a meal on her own except breakfast, and he had joined her three times even for that.

He could stand very still, and could also move with unexpected, quick-silvery movements. When they were together, she doubted whether she made a move which he did not notice. She had gone to the studio less and less, and was using up her savings. Theo hardly seemed to think of money in the ordinary, everyday sense.

He let her go.

'Now, if you've finished supposing, we can continue with the conversation,' he said, 'and it's a waste of time, hon. I am going to buy that ring, and I am not going to wear it myself, and I am not going to put it in a vault, safe, strongroom, or museum, so you might as well get used to the idea that you're going to walk around some of the time with the Red Eye of Love right on your next-to-little finger.'

She faced him very steadily. She did not understand him now and wondered whether she ever would. She could not really believe in him. She knew only that he could make her laugh and as easily make her cry, that when he was with her, her heart exulted, and when he was not, she felt lost and alone. He always had his own way. It was obvious that he had never felt a restraining hand. The world was made for him, and he was going to see that it behaved the way he wanted it, and his years hadn't tempered his enthusiasm or his exuberance. She had protested about other extravagances, but they had all been trifling compared with this. Now, she knew that she was going to have to make him realise that she meant exactly what she said.

'Theo,' she said quietly.

'Was the fit all right, honey?'

'I shall not wear that ring, as an engagement ring, or for any reason at all.'

He seemed really startled by her firmness. 'Now, hon!'

'I mean it, and there's nothing you can do to make me change my mind. Now let's stop talking about it.' She was more than a little afraid that, if they kept on talking, he would blow up with one of those furious outbursts. He had done so with a man in a cocktail bar, and once when a man had come to his suite at the Panorama Hotel. He had taken the most luxurious suite in London's most luxurious hotel, and they had been looking at a television programme when the man had called. There had been just a brief exchange of words and then a tremendous eruption; for a few minutes she had been almost frightened, in case Theo killed the man. Again she had asked herself if he was living on his nerves because of some deep-rooted fear; or whether the pressure of his fabulous activities was making him mentally ill. She had never met a man who behaved with such arrogance, nor one who could be more endearing.

Now he went white about the lips. She could see that his teeth were clenching. That was how he had looked before the earlier outbursts.

She felt almost despairing, because she did not see how she could prevent another.

Chapter Four

Persuasion

Rosamund thought Theo was going to bellow at her. His lips worked, and his fists clenched and were raised a little. He began to rise and fall on his toes, like an animal about to spring. She met his storming eyes without flinching, but inwardly she was afraid; and her heartbeats seemed to suffocate her.

Then, like a whirlwind, he swung round towards the window. He reached it in a few strides, and stood with his back towards her, staring at the High Street, the passing traffic, a clock in a church tower. She could hear him breathing, could hear the thumping of her own heart: that was all. The squareness of his shoulders, the erectness of his carriage, were so much a part of him that she wanted to break down, run towards him, and tell him she would take the ring, would take anything he wanted to give her. But she stayed there because she felt that this was a supreme test: to make or break the love between them.

Slowly, he turned round.

For him to do anything slowly was remarkable.

He smiled at her.

'I don't see why we should quarrel, hon,' he said, in a relaxed voice; and his expression and his body had relaxed too. 'I'm just going to hope that you change your mind. Maybe you don't believe that I want you to have that ring because it's the only way I can show you how much I love you. That's the simple truth. It's a kind of love token.' He came nearer, and she realised that he hadn't given up; he would never give up trying to get or do whatever he wanted; but now he was intent on persuading her. It must have been a tormenting struggle within himself, but he'd won it.

'Just tell me one thing,' he went on, standing very close to her. 'You don't believe that nonsense about the legend, do you?'

She was puzzled. 'What legend?'

'You mean you don't know about it?'

'All I know is what was in the *Collector and Connoisseur*. When you said you were going to get me the finest engagement ring in the world I wondered what you were talking about, and then I saw the book opened at the page describing the Red Eye of Love.'

He gave her a quick, almost impersonal hug, and swung away from her. 'Gee, honey, you've got a surprise coming to you. You don't know about that legend? It was one of the first things I was told when I began to inquire about it. That article was all facts and figures. D'you know what my gentleman friend Mannering would say? He would say that it hadn't any romance. No heart.' He thumped the left side of his chest. 'Not like me! It forgot history. Come and sit down and listen to me.' He dropped into a large armchair and patted his lap, and, half laughing, she went to him and he pulled her down, kissed her almost perfunctorily, and hugged her.

'This ring was made for a Babylonian babe, way, way back in Bee Cee. She was a beauty but as cold as ice. No red blood, no fire in the eye or passion in the bosom. Well, the then big shot of Babylon wanted to break her down, if you see what I mean. So he made a deal with her pa, and they got married. It was like marrying an Egyptian mummy, only they weren't mummifying 'em then. Like lying in bed with a lump of ice, say. Some guys would have given up, put her in a nice big country house all on her own where she could see the view, and fixed himself a cosy harem in the city. But not this kingpin. He didn't like being beaten. I've known other guys like that,' digressed Theo, and squeezed her until she gasped. 'So he decided he was going to woo and win this dame he'd wedded. He showered gifts on her, gave her slaves by the dozen, and diamonds by the thousand, she had only to lift her little finger and half Babylon would come running. But NBG. No blooming go.'

'So what did he do?'

'He had this very ring made, the Red Eye of Love. The story goes that there was the centre diamond with a reputation already made, a red diamond which warmed the old cockles and acted like a love philtre. He got this stone. He made the ring, the finest ring then ever known to man. Next he gave it to the icicle as a present, and sat back to see if it worked.' Theo broke off.

Rosamund had found herself listening intently, instead of laughing at his airy disrespect for phraseology and history. She stared at him, and he wrinkled his nose. Teasing. She was eager to know what was supposed to have happened, and he knew that she was.

'Well, go on!'

'Want to know if it worked?'

'Of course I do.'

'Oh boy, oh boy, did it work! There's never been a love philtre like it. First of all, she had twins. Then a couple of boys. Then there was a police action somewhere around the eastern end of the old Mediterranean, and Kingpin marched off to war, leaving little Wifey and the family behind, with a lot of courtiers and strong-arm men to look after her. Which they did. It worked so well that Kingpin came back from the wars, heard a thing or two, chopped off a few heads, and gave Wifey a dish of poison. He also buried the Red Eye of Love so deep that no one was ever going to find it, but wind and erosion and maybe soil subsidence settled his hash over that, and it was found in 1889 during some excavations there. And those excavations weren't for relics, honey, they were for oil. How about that?'

'I'd hate to be given a dish of poison,' Rosamund said in a small voice. 'What happened then?'

'Phooh, you don't want to worry your head about that.'

'I want to know what happened then,' said Rosamund, and struggled to get up. He held her fast for a moment, but soon let her go, and she stretched her cramped legs, then sat on the arm of his chair, resting a hand on his shoulder.

'The story goes that it was bought by a South American millionaire for his lady love, and she went off with another,' Theo declared. 'He sold out to an Indian prince. The potentate gave it to his daughter, who had so many admirers she didn't marry anyone. It went back to the little old United States and was bought by an ancient Texan millionaire who'd fallen in love with a young and lovely little minx who wouldn't say yes. When he gave it to her, she did say "aye", and they lived happily ever after. At least, their marriage was happy ever after, until she poisoned him and ran off and married a younger, more handsome man. The trouble was that by then the police knew a thing or two about the effects of poison. Next, Red Eye was bought by another millionaire for its own sake, and put in a collection. The collection was broken up, and the ring was given to a girl who married an Englishman. That's where I'm going to disappoint you,' added Theo with an impish grin. 'That marriage was ideal, but family fortunes suffered, and the ring was sold. Get it?'

'Then Mannering bought it?' Rosamund suggested.

'Yip!' said Theo, and jumped up from his chair. 'He bought it. I've been checking on that guy; he certainly is a private eye worth knowing. Scion of nobility, ran out of luck, family lost a fortune, looked as if he was out for the count, began to deal in precious stones, soon made a fortune. Well, what he'd call a fortune.' Theo flung that remark out carelessly. 'Married the daughter of an earl who made his money in trade, shocking thing! She's a painter; got quite a reputation in her own right. Name of Lorna – supposed to be the tops.'

He broke off.

A new and different glittering light appeared in his eyes, and he began to nod, very slowly. Then he went on, 'Sure, that's right.' Then he added: 'It's a humdinger; it's a dandy.' He put his head on one side and studied her. 'Turn your head a little that way,' he said and frowned, and then ordered, 'Look upwards a little, raise your head – hold it! Hold it!' he repeated, and slapped his hands. 'That's perfect!' He swung round towards the telephone which was near the fireplace, and before she realised what he was doing, was flipping over the pages of the directory. 'Main – Mai – Man,' he crooned. 'Mannering, John, 24 Green Street, SW3. Flaxman ...' He began to dial, as Rosamund jumped off the chair and ran towards him.

'Theo, don't!'

'Don't crowd me, honey,' he said, and fended her off with one hand as he held the instrument to his ear. She could just make out the ringing sound, then a sharp break, and a vague voice.

'I want to talk to Mrs John Mannering,' Theo said crisply, but it was the glint in his eyes, a kind of radiance and a look almost of exaltation on his face which fascinated Rosamund. It made her stand still, watching, thinking that his must be the most vital face in the world. 'What is? ... Fine! ... Mrs Mannering, I've got an order for you, a wotcher-callit – a commission, that's right. I want the best portrait ever painted of my fiancée, and for the real goods, the sky's the limit ... Yes, ma'am, you couldn't be more right, I'm serious ... Yes, ma'am ... What did you say?' He broke off. He looked flabbergasted, opened his mouth, closed it again, gulped, and let the receiver sag from his ear.

There was a woman's voice, sounding very faintly, and it stopped.

'Yes, that's right, I am Theodorus Wray,' he said, in a whisper. 'Yes, ma'am, how ... Oh, sure. Sure I understand ... That's right, ma'am.' His voice strengthened a little. 'I'd like that, Mrs Mannering.' His eyes brightened. 'Yes, ma'am, that'll be dandy, we'll be there. Six-forty-five, yes, ma'am!' He was quite himself again. 'Formal dress, yes, ma'am! Now don't ring off, just wait a minute.' He clapped a hand over the receiver and beamed at Rosamund, but ignored her when she asked urgently, 'What is it?' He was looking at her reflectively.

Then he said into the telephone, 'Mrs Mannering, I'll be glad if you'll tell John that I'd like him to have the Red Eye of Love with him tonight. I've got a feeling my fiancée is going to change her mind. Thank you ... Thank you, ma'am!' He rang off.

'Theo, I t—told you—' Rosamund began, but her exasperation was tempered by curiosity, and she stammered over the words.

Theo looked at her with a great light in his eyes. 'That's what I call dandy, honey! We're having dinner with the Mannerings tonight.

Just imagine. Poor boy makes good, dines with English aristos in their own home. That's progress. That's the kind of progress you only dream about. Anybody can make money—' He broke off, thrust out his arms, took Rosamund by the shoulders, and stood her at arm's length, his gaze running all over her slim body. 'Honey, I'm going to buy you the most expensive cocktail gown and the most expensive dinner gown there is in London. We don't have much time.'

'But he's fantastic,' Lorna Mannering said, and found herself laughing. She was in Mannering's office a little before one o'clock, on her way to lunch with the agent who handled her paintings. 'Even over the telephone he had a way with him.' She went on, 'I really think he expected me to drop everything and start on this girl of his. What is she like?'

Mannering, sitting on the corner of his desk, looked up at his wife with a smile. Lorna was sitting in his chair behind the desk, wearing a mink bolero and a small black hat trimmed with mink, and looking rather as if she had just stepped out of the pages of *Vogue*.

'Not so lovely as you were twenty years ago,' Mannering declared, 'but still worth putting everything aside and painting her.'

'You sound almost as if you believe it.'

'What is it the French say?' Mannering mused aloud. 'Good as bread. That isn't quite right, but it gives you an idea. She has a look of virtue, whatever she's really like, and it shows. You'll take one peek at her, and your fingers will itch to start work.'

'I'm glad I arranged to see this remarkable young woman,' said Lorna dryly, but her blue eyes were laughing. 'Wray was shaken when I guessed who he was; I'm glad you'd telephoned before he came through. I have a feeling that I'd like to take him down a peg or two.'

'He'll bob up if you do,' said Mannering. 'He's quite irrepressible. He has an astounding reputation too. I've checked with the Yard and with Peggotty, of United Oils. He's absolutely genuine, and wherever he goes he makes a fortune. He owns huge stretches of iron ore land in Australia, which he's fond of calling his homeland; a lot of uranium deposits in South Africa and the African colonies; oil in South America, North Africa, Canada and'—Mannering found himself chuckling—'actually in Texas! He bought up about twenty thousand acres of land which had been drilled and found useless, and struck oil within two months. If ever there was a man with the Midas touch, it's Theo Wray. Guess how old he is.'

'Fifty-five?'

'Nearer forty-five,' said Mannering. 'He does nearly everything by himself, except that he's got a secretary-cum-body-guard named Charley. Real name, Charles Simpson. As far as I can trace he's never been seriously involved with a woman, until this girl bowled him over. There are one or two stories told about the way a Hollywood stripper and a British blonde tried to inveigle him, and he stepped right out without batting an eye, but Rosamund Morrel's different.'

'How old is she?'

'Oh – twenty-five or six,' Mannering guessed.

'Is she as genuine as you seem to think?' murmured Lorna.

'No one seems to know much about her,' Mannering said. 'They met at a cocktail party thrown by an old friend of Theo's. The Press was along in strength, and Chitty tells me that he knows that half a dozen of the Soho boys were there with their girl friends, but no one made any impression on Theo except this girl.'

'Who took her along?' asked Lorna, standing up and taking her gloves from the corner of his desk. She was only half a head shorter than Mannering, and looked many years younger than she was.

'As far as Chitty knows, she was taken by a friend who does a gossip column in one of the women's weeklies. She's still a bit of a mystery, but there hasn't been much time to solve it. There has been time to find out that our office Thomas would gladly let her walk over him to keep her feet dry.'

'After one meeting?' Lorna looked wary. 'I shall keep a close eye on you.' She put her face up, and Mannering kissed her lightly. 'Don't be later home than half past five; you've got to change. When I said formal dress, he seemed overjoyed.'

Mannering chuckled.

'Will you take the Red Eye of Love?' Lorna asked, a little uncertainly, and when Mannering didn't answer at once, added rather hurriedly, 'I'm never happy when you have jewels like that at the flat. If you're going to, I'd like to have someone watching, to make sure there isn't any bother.'

'I'll be taking it,' Mannering said, 'and there won't be any bother.'

'If that ring were stolen—'

'It isn't going to be stolen,' Mannering assured her firmly. 'You'll be late if you don't hurry.'

Lorna went out, but obviously wasn't easy in her mind. Mannering went to the door of Hart Row with her, passing Thomas, who stood almost at attention. She was only five minutes' walk away from her rendezvous, and went off briskly.

As Mannering turned back into the shop, a telephone bell rang. He heard Larraby announce, 'This is Quinns,' in his gentle voice, and as he reached the office, Larraby looked up. 'It's Mr Chittering, sir.'

'Thanks,' said Mannering, 'I'll take it here.' He took the receiver from Larraby's hand, said, 'Hello, Chitty,' and wondered what the crime reporter of the *Daily Globe* would have to tell him now.

He felt sure that it would be something about Theodorus Wray.

Chapter Five

Bristow Of The Yard

'John,' said Chittering, in a deep voice which was obviously calculated to impress, 'I have shattering news for you.'

'I can bear it, provided you don't tell me that Theo Wray is a fake.'

'He's no fake; he's a man of flesh and oil. His little Rosamund has some odd friends, though.'

'Oh,' said Mannering, and felt a twinge of disappointment, although, from the moment he had met her, he had accepted the possibility that Rosamund Morrel was a little too perfect to be true. 'Such as?'

'Micky Odell.'

'Oh,' repeated Mannering, in a very different tone of voice – the tone that a man might use if he had been told that he had lost a fortune. 'Sure they're associates?'

'Nice distinction,' Chittering chuckled. 'I know for certain that she has been to several cocktail parties with him. They're not close friends, but they often run around in the same kind of group. It's true that not all of Micky's group are as black as Micky, but those who touch dirt get dirty, don't they?'

'Can you find out more?' said Mannering. 'I'd hate Wray to be taken for a ride.'

'I've already found out more,' Chittering assured him. 'From the time that Theodorus Wray came into this country, he was taken under the wing of an old friend, a school buddy, one of the few people he's kept in touch with. This chap, Norman Kilham, is a City accountant, and he's looked after some of Wray's interests here. He has a sound reputation, but recently he's been working for Micky Odell. Micky is known to be on the borderline of income and surtax trouble, and this Norman Kilham has kept him in the clear. On the surface, it's simply a professional association, but Micky doesn't usually give business to anyone but buddies. So Norman Kilham threw a cocktail party, and two or three of Micky's crowd were there, including Rosamund Morrel – if we can say that she's of the crowd. It seems to add up.'

'It could,' agreed Mannering.

'Micky sent the loveliest of the luscious things he keeps in tow,' went on Chittering brightly. 'Vital statistics all in order, cleavage according to custom. Rosamund was odd girl out; she doesn't rely on statistics for her sex appeal, and nearly always wears high-necked dresses. It looks to me as if Micky Odell tried to make sure that one of them got their hooks into the modern Midas, and that sooner or later Theo Wray would lose a lot of money.'

'Could be,' mused Mannering. 'Can you check the girl anymore?'

'I'm checking. So,' went on Chittering, with a laugh in his voice, 'is Scotland Yard. They're keeping an eye on Wray now that they know Micky Odell is interested, because there's no one they'd love to get their claws into more than Micky. It's all being done very carefully, of course. Micky himself is still right in the background.'

'I see,' said Mannering. 'Thanks, Chitty.'

'You mind your little pieces of coloured glass. If Micky Odell is very interested he might try to take some of them away,' Chittering warned. 'He's a man of catholic tastes. All he asks is that what he collects should be worth a lot of money.'

Mannering smiled as he rang off.

He went into his office, sat at his desk, and looked up at a picture of a laughing cavalier on the wall opposite, and so looked into a face that was the image of his own ten years ago. Then he plucked up the telephone, dialled Whitehall 1212, and asked for Superintendent Bristow.

'One moment, sir,' the Scotland Yard operator said.

One moment grew into many. Someone came into the shop and Larraby went forward to wait on him. The Red Eye of Love, temporarily in a small safe built into Mannering's desk and unsuspected by most people, seemed to be on the desk, looking at him as if it was in fact an eye. Then William Bristow, one of the Yard's senior superintendents, came on the line.

'Did I get it right? That you, John?'

'Your chaps are getting almost efficient,' Mannering said dryly. 'Yes, Bill. Hungry?'

'I was just going across to the pub for lunch.'

'How about meeting me at the Club?'

'Sorry,' Bristow said, 'but I have to be on tap; one or two jobs are pending. They can fetch me from the pub.'

'Think they'll let me in there too?'

'I'll use my influence.'

'I'll be there in twenty minutes,' said Mannering. 'If you care to let yourself ponder over Theodorus Wray, his lady love and friends—'

'So that's it,' Bristow said dryly. 'I'll look forward to seeing you.'

Mannering went out, leaving Larraby talking to a middle-aged, yellow-skinned man from Iraq, who had come to sell and not to buy, and Thomas and Sylvester with a swarthy Venezuelan millionaire and his sultry wife, who had come to buy. Mannering took a taxi, and was soon held up in a traffic block.

He wondered whether it would have been quicker to walk, but at least he had time for a little reflection. Bristow had given nothing away, but that wasn't surprising. Bristow was both an old friend and old adversary: there wasn't a shrewder man at the Yard. No one in the police knew as much about precious stones.

Mannering turned into the dining room of the public house in Cannon Row, only a step from New Scotland Yard. He looked round, saw that nearly everyone noticed him, and many nudged, then espied Bristow sitting alone in a corner. He went across, and Bristow stood up, a lean man of middle age, quite grey hair cut short, good-looking in a curiously inanimate way. His grey eyes held a smile as he shook hands.

He was immaculately dressed: the Yard's dandy. In his coat lapel was a white gardenia which was not showing the slightest sign of fading. His grey moustache was stained yellow to dark brown with nicotine, and he had a cigarette alight on an ashtray on the table.

A waitress came up.

As they ordered steak-and-kidney pudding, beer in pewter tankards appeared before them as if by magic. They let the froth settle while they chatted about wives, business, the Government, income tax, and cricket, then drank deeply and launched immediately into the topic most on Mannering's mind.

'I hear that Theodorus Wray wants to buy the Red Eye for this Morrel girl, and so far she hasn't let him do it,' Bristow said.

'Someone must have been talking.'

'Chittering, for one,' said Bristow, 'and we're watching Wray. We had a chap in Hart Row this morning, and when the ring was taken out of the window—' He shrugged. Soup arrived, steaming hot and thick. 'Ah,' he went on, and picked up his spoon. 'I'm famished.'

Mannering was hungry too, but Bristow had hardly finished dabbing his lips before he went on, 'Do you know that Micky Odell seems interested, and that an accountant named Kilham, an old school friend of Wray's, works for Odell?'

'Yes.'

'I don't think there's a man in the country we'd rather put inside than Micky Odell,' Bristow said earnestly. 'He's run his racket for so long that you'd think he would have slipped up by now, but he's as careful today as he was when he began five years ago.' There was a glint almost of admiration in Bristow's voice. 'He's got some of the loveliest girls in London working for him, and his method's always the same. They find the rich fool to work on, and get expensive presents like diamond necklaces and all kinds of jewellery out of him. When they've fleeced the old fool enough they give him the air. Micky handles the sale of their loot, so that everyone except the victim is satisfied. But there's one odd thing.'

The waitress brought their steak-and-kidney pudding. The steaming brown meat brought a glint to Bristow's eyes. 'Always did make good puddings at this place,' he remarked. 'Just as good as pre-war.' He tucked in, his enthusiasm fading only when the plate was nearly empty. 'Now, where was I?'

'You were talking about an odd thing,' Mannering prompted.

Bristow screwed up his face. 'Odd thing, odd thing, odd thing. Oh, yes! When we started looking into Mickey Odell's activities, we thought he was on a different kind of racket, call-girl angle, that kind of thing. But he isn't. All the girls he uses are show-girls or models with good reputations. Nothing morally nasty about it at all. He has them at his cocktail parties, he introduces them to the victim, who makes his own choice, and doesn't use any pressure as far as I can find out.'

'Kind words from a hardhearted cop.'

'Never did see any point in exaggerating or blinking at facts,' said Bristow, and paused while he finished the pudding. He sat back and sipped his beer. 'Mind if I smoke?' He was beginning to light up already, remembered to offer cigarettes, then went on. 'Odell relies on the oldest law of all: that the man who makes a fool of himself doesn't want to admit it. The few who have complained to the police haven't been able to supply evidence of specific crime, but we don't like to feel that Micky Odell is laughing at us. We're pretty sure he deals in other stolen jewels too. But you know that as well as I do.'

'I know he's a good judge of precious stones,' said Mannering mildly. 'I wouldn't like to go any further, Bill. Sure that Rosamund Morrel is one of his decoy birds?'

'No,' replied Bristow, 'but she's been going to these cocktail parties on and off for nearly a year. She's not the ordinary type, of course – all my chaps who've seen her say they think that Micky's saving her for a really special client. No one could be more special than Theodorus Wray.'

The waitress came up, and Bristow looked at the menu, frowned, hesitated, and said, 'Fruit salad, cheese and biscuits, or jam roll. Oh, to hell with my waistline, jam roll. John?'

'I'll have a piece of Camembert,' Mannering said.

'Just as fattening,' declared Bristow, who looked as if he hadn't a spare ounce of flesh on him. 'Where do you come in on this?'

'Only as the man who owns the ring that Wray wants for his girl friend,' said Mannering. 'I should say Wray's deeply in love with the girl, the way a man in his forties will fall for the young and the lovely. I should hate to sell the ring to him if he's going to be fleeced as well as disappointed in Rosamund.'

'Nice to know you're so civic-minded,' said Bristow, and rubbed his hands as the baked jam roll, its rich golden pastry oozing red jam and thick custard, was placed in front of him. 'If you can help us to stop Micky Odell's little game, we'll strike a special medal for you.'

'First we want to know exactly what the little game is,' observed Mannering. Then he chuckled, enough to make Bristow stop eating. 'I wonder if the simple thing wouldn't be to turn Theo loose on Micky Odell. The result could be spectacular.'

Bristow nodded, went back to eating, was reflectively slow until he said thoughtfully, 'Be interesting to see if the Morrel girl accepts the ring. If she does, then we can say her earlier refusals have been phony, just to make Wray more eager. And also to make sure that the world knows it was a free gift,' he added, almost gloomily.

'Think she'll take it?'

'I'll know before the night's out,' Mannering said, and finished the ripe Camembert.

Chapter Six

One Man's Fury

'Come away from the window,' Mannering said to Lorna, 'it's not yet twenty-five past.'

'It wouldn't have surprised me if he'd arrived early,' Lorna said. 'He gave me the impression that he couldn't get here fast enough.' She continued to stare out of the window into Green Street, and Mannering joined her, carrying her gin, and his own whisky and soda. She was wearing a dark green cocktail dress, off the shoulder but with a high neckline. She had lovely shoulders, and her dark hair, with a few strands of grey, was luxuriant and had a natural wave. She wore a green jade necklace and green jade earrings.

'Here they are!' she exclaimed as a car turned into the street and slowed down.

'Not on your life,' said Mannering. "Theo will come in his scarlet Cadillac, and turn that corner on two wheels.' He stared with idle curiosity at the other car, a one-and-a-half litre Jaguar, but he couldn't see the driver, couldn't even be sure how many people were in the car. It pulled up a little way along, where there was an empty patch of land, for many of the houses in this terrace had been demolished by bombing, and had still not been replaced. There were rumours that a block of mansion flats was to be erected here. If it were true, the Mannerings would soon have to move.

A man got out of the car.

He was young, small, and well-dressed in pale grey, and his sleek dark hair seemed to shine in the evening sun. So did his brown shoes. He strolled towards this house and looked upwards, an ordinary enough fellow, except for the unmistakable cut and quality of his clothes.

He could not see the Mannerings, although they could see him.

'Chitty would say he's casing the joint,' Mannering murmured.

Lorna looked round. 'Do you think he is?'

'Let's assume that there won't be any trouble,' Mannering said. 'Josh has put our Tom downstairs, and a man at the back into the bargain, just to soothe your fears.'

Lorna said thanks by squeezing his hand.

Then she looked towards the corner, and Mannering stared, too. For another car had arrived. It was not the Cadillac, but Mannering felt quite sure that it was Theodorus Wray's. This was a Rolls Bentley in a dual tone of grey, a beautiful car with superb lines. It turned the corner with the grace of an antelope, and although it moved quite fast, there was nothing jolty or jerky. It slowed down as it neared the house.

The little man from the Jaguar stood only a few yards away.

Lorna shot an anxious glance at Mannering. 'Oh, what a nuisance he's there, I want to see Theo.'

'There he is,' said Mannering.

Theodorus Wray climbed out of the Rolls Bentley. He wore a pale mauve tuxedo and black or dark blue trousers, and compared with him the little man looked as if his clothes had been bought off the peg. Wray appeared for a moment, so foreshortened that they could only see the top of his head, and his short hair – going thin on top, it proved. Then he leaned inside the back of the car; obviously Rosamund was there.

She appeared, a vision in scarlet. She looked so vividly beautiful that it seemed to light up and give fire to the drab grey street.

Lorna caught her breath, and as the girl stood by Wray's side, she breathed, 'What a beautiful dress! Oh, John, and that girl. Why didn't you tell me?'

Something made Rosamund look up, so that both of them could see her. This dress was also high at the neck, but sleeveless; that showed as she adjusted the light wrap. Her hair looked jet black against the red, and the whiteness of her shoulders.

'She's come straight out of a Botticelli,' Lorna said, as if overawed.

Mannering did not speak, for he had not been studying the girl or Theodorus: he had been watching the perky little man who now seemed almost shabby. This man had one hand in his pocket, and stood almost aggressively, watching the couple.

In the front room of a downstairs flat, Thomas of Quinns was standing by the window, on guard because the Red Eye of Love was in Mannering's flat, and no one must come near unless they could be vouched for.

The stranger drew nearer the couple.

Mannering saw him speak.

Theodorus Wray took his arm off the girl's. She put a hand on his, as if trying to keep him close to her; something in her manner suggested that she was pleading with him. She actually tried to drag him back as he went towards the little man, who stood with his right hand in his pocket, shoulders squared in a kind of defiance.

Lorna's hand was tight about Mannering's arm. 'What's he going to do?'

'I don't know.'

'Has he got a gun?' Lorna was breathless.

'Tom's at the window,' Mannering reminded her.

'That won't be any use if—' Lorna began, and broke off with a catch at her breath.

Theodorus Wray was taking a long, slow step one moment, and going forward like a rocket the next. The little man snatched his hand out of his pocket, and a dark weapon showed: not a gun or a knife, but a leather cosh. He had no time to raise it, before Wray was upon him, fists moving like pistons. The little man gave ground and tried to turn and run, but could not turn away. Then a second man, much larger, jumped out of the Jaguar and flung himself at Wray.

Lorna exclaimed, 'He'll kill him!'

Rosamund obviously saw the second man coming, and actually went forward as if to intercept, but, in a flurry of movement so fast that it was hard to be sure exactly what happened, the perky little man crashed down at full length. Wray turned to meet the second, larger man, who also carried a weapon, which looked like a length of rubber piping. He made one sweeping blow with it, aimed at Wray's head, and missed by inches. Next moment he must have felt as if he had been hit by an elephant, for he went staggering back until he flopped down. He banged his head on the pavement, and lay very still.

Thomas of Quinns appeared from the house, running furiously.

'You're late, Tom,' Mannering murmured. 'I think you'll nearly always be late for Theo Wray.'

Wray had turned from the two fallen men, the larger of whom still lay there, while the other tried to scramble to his feet. Neither of them appeared to exist for Wray. He rubbed his hands together, then flexed his fingers, slid his arm through Rosamund Morrel's, and led her to the front door.

She seemed to go with him as if she'd no will of her own, as if she were floating.

'It's a pity Theo decided to turn his talents to making money,' Mannering murmured, and his voice was a little strained. 'He would have been the best British boxer since Jimmy Wilde. Well, we can leave Tom to pick up the pieces.' He finished his drink. 'Come and pretend you didn't notice a thing; let's see how they behave when they get here.'

Lorna finished her gin and Italian, and said, 'Make my next one stronger,' and looked at herself in the Georgian mirror over the drawing-room mantelpiece, and poked her hair about; but she did it half-heartedly.

There was a lift, quite recently installed; any moment the front-door bell would ring, and Claudia, their maid of six months, would open the door and then come and announce them: for Claudia was in her sixties, and knew what service was.

The front-door bell rang.

Mannering looked at Lorna and chuckled. 'I haven't known you so much on edge for years, not since we first had Bill Bristow here.'

'Be quiet, you fool!'

The door opened, and grey-haired Claudia appeared and announced as if she was announcing royalty, 'Miss Rosamund Morrel and Mr Theodorus Wray.'

Theo came in, with Rosamund on his arm. Rosamund looked a little pale, but Theodorus not only came fresh as from a bandbox, but was smiling as if determined to reveal the brightest, most dazzling smile in the world. His hair looked as if nothing had disturbed it. There was not a wrinkle on that pale mauve coat, his shirt, or his dark navy bow tie, which was very narrow. The studs at the shirt were obviously of diamonds, but they were not ostentatious.

'Hi, John.' He came forward with hand outstretched, gripped Mannering's, then slapped him with his free hand across the shoulder. He turned to Lorna, and contrived to put a kind of electric radiance into his smile as he took her hand. 'I guess you're Lorna. It's swell meeting you. I want you to meet the most beautiful girl in the world.'

He thrust a hand towards Rosamund, like a boxing referee indicating the winner of a closely fought fight. Rosamund looked embarrassed, yet was smiling. She had to take Theodorus as he was, so everyone else had to.

Lorna expected Theodorus to crush her hand. Instead, he just held it firmly.

Lorna had already caught a vision of this girl, but realised now, as Rosamund stood with her cheeks slightly flushed and in that glorious scarlet gown, that few could even begin to imagine beauty like it.

'Well, I guess your shop manager wouldn't come and work for me, so it's no use trying to bribe your cook away,' Theo said, and the broad, bright smile which accompanied the words made Lorna and Mannering laugh, and made Wray seem as likeable as a man could be. 'This place is wonderful. Maybe it doesn't look much like an ancestral home from the outside, but when you get in here and see some of these antiques – shades of Texas and New South Wales!

Gives me a new outlook on a lot of things, John. I guess I'm going to be the biggest customer you ever had. But that can wait. I've got something else that can't wait. I don't know how I've managed to be so patient since we arrived.'

He looked at Mannering.

They were back in the drawing room, a room of blues and golds and Regency furniture, of beautiful portraits, including a Gainsborough and two by Lorna Fauntley, now Lorna Mannering. It was large and charming, and the Adam fireplace gave the rest of it a kind of gracefulness which reached to every corner and to the high ceiling.

Mannering stood by Lorna's chair; Rosamund was sitting on a stool near the fireplace where a fire glowed, for the evening was chilly. Theo stood between her and Mannering, with that light of challenge in his eyes.

'Theo—' Rosamund began, as if pleadingly.

'Do you have the Red Eye of Love right here?' Theo asked.

'Theo, please,' Rosamund said.

'Just leave this to me, honey.'

'Are you sure you won't have a cigar, or a cigarette?' Lorna asked, in a forlorn attempt to change the subject.

'No, thank you, I don't smoke,' said Theo. 'It always seemed to me crazy to burn money. But I've got a fat little corner in Rhodesian tobacco, and one of these days I'm going right down to dear li'l old Virginny.' His smile flashed as he turned back to Mannering. 'Do you have that ring, John?'

Mannering looked at Rosamund, who raised her hands and shrugged, as if to say, 'It's no use; he'd better have it.'

'Yes,' Mannering said, and slipped his hand into his trousers' pocket and drew out a beautifully made case of Moroccan leather.

'Why, you've had it right next to me all the time!' Theo exclaimed. 'I hand it to you, John. May I have it?'

Mannering snatched a glance at Rosamund, and thought of what Bristow had said at lunch time. Then he heard Lorna breathe in sharply, as if she had winced at the sight of the ring. All expression except a kind of wonder vanished from Rosamund's eyes. Theo took her left hand and placed the ring on the engagement finger, just as he had that morning.

There was a difference now.

The scarlet of the dress seemed to be reflected in the centre diamond, so that it glowed a deeper red; and as it slid gently upon her finger, the whole of the ring seemed to become alive, to breathe and sparkle like a beautiful woman.

'Now it's on again, and I don't want you to take it off until you agree that it's the ring with which we plight our troth,' said Theo.

His voice was almost humble, and his eyes were pleading.

Chapter Seven

Decision

Rosamund knew that both Mannering and his wife were watching her intently, yet she was aware only of the ring blazing on her finger, and of the appeal in Theo's eyes. He seemed to be begging her to accept the ring, to make it an issue of her love for him. His hands, which could be so vigorous, and sometimes squeezed her until it hurt, were just as firm now; he was oblivious of the Mannerings, of all the world but their two selves.

She was positive of that.

Reason told her that this was a kind of madness, that no woman should wear a ring which was both fortune and history on her hand. Thought of the possession of it gave her a choky feeling; as did thought of her love for him.

He did not speak again, obviously anxious not to break a spell.

But gradually his fingers tightened, as if he were trying to force the words he longed to hear from her. It was useless to tell herself that it was madness, really a kind of exhibitionism, that he had made a fetish of having only the best, for her and for himself: it was as hard to believe that it was not a love token, but a mark of his own arrogant self-esteem, another indication that, whatever he wanted, he could get. All these things might be true, but the only realities were the fire in the ring and the worship in his eyes and the pressure of his fingers.

She was going to say yes.

He sensed it; there must have been something in the movement of her body, perhaps the way she drew in her breath. Whatever it was, he sensed it even before she formed the word. Suddenly she could not form words, because of the pressure of his lips on hers, and his devouring strength.

Then he let her go. 'Honey,' he said, 'I'm the happiest man in this world.'

Mannering felt Lorna touching him as they watched the couple. It would be easy to laugh, because she seemed to be willing Rosamund to say yes, seemed to be drawn into the vortex of the couple's emotions, as she might be at a play or a film, where disbelief was suspended and the players were playing out their own brief drama of love.

Her eyes were glowing when Theo took the girl in his arms.

Mannering gave Lorna an understanding squeeze.

She looked round, and he saw the suspicion of a tear at her eyes, but didn't scoff. There was sentiment and there was emotion; this was the real stuff of emotion.

Then Theo drew back, let the girl go, and said in a quiet voice, 'Honey, I'm the happiest man in this world.'

He turned round briskly, holding both hands outstretched, and gave a little quirk of a smile as he said, 'John, you couldn't run to champagne, could you?'

'I believe we could for an occasion like this,' Mannering said. 'Darling, come and help me find it.' He drew Lorna out of the drawing room. She closed the door, gave a little laugh, and said, 'I've never really believed in people being made for each other before.'

Mannering put his head on one side. 'I think I resent that.'

'How long do you think we ought to leave them together?'

'Half an hour will seem like thirty seconds.'

'I suppose so. Well, you get the champagne – it's up in the studio – and I'll get the glasses. I don't suppose Claudia knows where they are; we haven't had champagne since she came.' Lorna moved towards the kitchen, and Mannering towards the approach to the bathroom and the loft ladder which led up to the studio. But she came hurrying after him, in alarm. 'John, I've just remembered the fight outside. What do you think that was all about?'

'I want to find out.'

'Theo looked as if he would have killed the man.'

'He probably knows where to draw the line,' Mannering said. 'I wonder how they knew that he was coming here. Would he have told the world?'

'What do you mean?'

'If he didn't tell anyone else, who did?'

'You mean, did Rosamund?'

'She could have.'

'I think Theo was in a mood where he could have told the first person he came across,' Lorna asserted, 'but—oh, forget it. You're as bad as Bristow and Larraby. Why on earth must you suspect that the girl is setting out to cheat Theo? Have you ever seen anything more genuine than her hesitation about the ring?'

'I've never known anything look so genuine.'

'I think she's perfectly honest, and that she loves him so much that it hurts, even if he is twenty years older,' Lorna said. 'I'll be surprised if they're not married within the next week or two. Now go and get the champagne, and stop thinking that Rosamund Morrel is a Delilah.' When Mannering didn't respond, she added thoughtfully, 'Of course, I could get to know her better. If she were here every day for a week, sitting for her portrait …'

'You're going to get to know her better, anyhow; that's exactly what our Theo wants,' Mannering reminded her.

He went up to the studio, with many canvases round the walls and two on easels, its smell of oil paint and turps, its old paint-daubed smock, its memories of their early married life. Lorna had had that breathtaking look of innocence too. Innocence? Mannering wished that there was no murmur of association between this girl and Mickey Odell. He was puzzled for many reasons, few of which he could explain. There was the girl and the causes for suspicion and the fact that her manner and appearance seemed to laugh suspicion away. There was Wray himself, the original human dynamo, a man who obviously knew nothing about precious stones, yet could feel the power of that red diamond.

Red!

Rose-pink, Mannering reminded himself; he was letting his imagination run away with him. The colour of the dress, almost certainly chosen by Theo, had turned pink to flaming red, and it had looked as if the touch of the girl's finger had caused the metamorphosis. She could not have failed to see it, to feel that it was right for her.

Mannering unearthed the champagne, which was stored in bins in a small loft next to the studio, dusted off two bottles, and took them downstairs. Lorna was ready, with the glasses.

She carried them so that they rattled noisily, and Mannering kicked deliberately against a chair as he opened the door. When they went in, Theo was on his feet and turning round towards them, his eyes dazed with delight. Rosamund was sitting on a corner of the settee, radiant.

'I want the loudest pop a champagne bottle ever made when it was opened!' cried Theo, clapping his hands together. 'How about letting me open it, John? ... No, forget it! I was only joking; that's what people forget about me, I've a sense of humour.' He clapped his hands with a resounding bang. 'We're going to be married in a church in three weeks' time – three weeks on Monday – that'll give time for the banns to be called. Can you finish that portrait in three weeks, Lorna?'

Lorna said helplessly, 'What will you say if I say no?'

'Find a way to make you hurry,' Theo answered. 'Maybe the right way would be to ask who you're painting now, and persuade him or maybe her that he/she wants to go to the South of France for a week or two. Then I'd fix it. I can always fix things,' he added. 'There's nothing you can't get if you want it hard enough. It isn't just a question of money, either. Tell me, isn't that true? Have I mentioned money to you? Hi, honey! Wake up! You can't spend all the evening looking at that ring; you've social duty to attend.'

Rosamund looked almost guilty as she glanced up from the left hand.

The two men were together, an hour later, when Lorna and Rosamund were putting the finishing touches to their make-up before they went out to a nightclub; Theo would not listen to the suggestion that he and Rosamund should go alone.

'Theo,' Mannering said, 'that diamond is insured only while it's in my possession.'

'That ring's insured for all time; I paid the insurance premium this afternoon,' announced Theo bluffly. 'I was in time to arrange a transfer from my British funds to Quinns before three o'clock, when your bank closes. Also, I have the documents right here.' Theo took them out of the pocket of his immaculate jacket. 'You simply have to telephone your solicitors and your bank manager – I'm told you have their home telephone numbers – to know that it's okay.' When Mannering took the documents without a word, Theo shrugged as if to say they could forget all formalities.

Mannering glanced down at a copy of the draft: it was for seventy-five thousand pounds exactly.

'Let's go make whoopee,' Theo said restlessly. 'How long do you think they'll be?'

'Not long,' Mannering said. 'Do you want Rosamund to wear the ring tonight?'

'Too right I do!'

'A lot of people would do murder to get their hands on it.'

'You're telling me,' said Theo offhandedly. 'No one is going to murder anybody while I'm around – or while you're around, either. I've been—'

'I know, you've been checking on me,' said Mannering hastily. 'Who were the two men outside tonight?'

Theo took that well; there was only a tightening of his lips and a narrowing of his eyes. He went a little white round the nostril and lips too, but his voice didn't alter. 'So you saw that.'

'Yes.'

'You couldn't have had a better view if you'd had a seat in the bleachers,' Theo said, and shrugged as he did at nearly everything: abruptly. 'John, I've made a lot of fortunes. I've made them in a lot of places, I've made a lot of men too, and broken others. I couldn't help it – often I didn't even know them. If I'd known them, I would have told them to get out before they got hurt. But I didn't know them. I'm big business. I'm more than big business, I'm MONEY in capital letters. I'm not human. I don't have flesh and blood like ordinary people when I'm buying land or stocks. I'm a machine and I'm using cyphers. That's the beginning and the end of it – until some of the cyphers get hurt. Then they become flesh and blood. What I'm trying to say,' went on Theo very quietly, 'is that I make enemies. There's one kind of person who gets hurt and can find his peace only in hurting back. There's the kind who won't risk his own skin but hires others to do the rough stuff too. I'm used to them all. You don't have to worry about me.'

'If I'm worried,' Mannering said, 'it's about Rosamund.'

There was a long pause, and then, quite unexpectedly, Theo said, 'That's the hell of it.' He glanced towards the door, as if he hoped that Lorna and Rosamund wouldn't come in yet, and went on, 'I've kept my eyes open, John, and I've been around. You know how people get hurt? They get hurt through other people. You torture a man, like the Nazis did, the Japs did, the Ruskis did – or do they still? Does pain make the man talk? Not if he's tough. But you take the toughest man alive and work on his wife or a kid or someone he loves, and he cracks. Yes, sir, he cracks wide open. I guess that's not an original remark, but I never was an egghead and I'm never likely to be. Deeds, not words, that's my credo.

'I didn't intend to fall in love. For twenty years I told myself I was proof against it. I told myself I couldn't get hurt, and no one who mattered to me would get hurt because of me. And then I saw Rosamund. Okay, okay, I'd been working on a theory, I was a machine making a lot of little cyphers run around, and then I found there was some blood in my veins after all. Don't I know it. And don't I know that someone could try to hurt me by hurting Rosamund. And that someone could try to rob me by using her. Those guys outside. I've seen them before. They started work on me five days ago. They said they wanted a hundred thousand pounds, that's three hundred thousand bucks, or Rosamund would get hurt. I said if Rosamund got hurt, nothing would squeeze a dime out of me. Check. That's how it is. And that gets me around to the second thing I wanted to see you about, John. You're the best that come in private eyes. I don't want protection for myself, but for her.'

He glanced at the door again. Rosamund's voice sounded, so the women were coming out of the bedroom. His grin flashed, and he gripped Mannering's arm. 'We'll talk later! I just want ideas, to begin with. Nothing must happen to her.'

It was strange to look at him, because it was strange to believe that he could be frightened. For the first time, he looked his age.

As the others drew nearer, he watched the door. It opened wide, and Rosamund came in. She must have been aware that she looked unbelievably lovely: beauty born out of flame. The ring on her finger was the very heart of the fire. Mannering glanced at Theodorus.

The man looked as if he could go down on his knees to worship his Rosamund.

The doorman at the Signet Club stared at Rosamund and forgot to help Lorna out of the car. The cloakroom girl stood absolutely still, at sight of her. A waiter carrying a tray of coffee stopped as if someone had put on the brakes, and just looked. The head waiter, coming sedately forward to welcome the party, a man who knew Mannering and who treated him as one would treat a prince, simply raised his hands and then very slowly bent his white head. The bandleader, baton poised for a downbeat to the saxophones, held it there for three more beats, and so left the band to its own resources. The nearest saxophonist swayed. The floor was crowded, and at least six couples stopped dancing. Every waiter, every man, and every woman at the tables stopped whatever they were doing, just to look at Rosamund.

Theo was aware of all this, and took it as Rosamund's natural right. The world was hers and Theo Wray's.

The zenith came when they danced together. Everyone looked their way, and the Signet Club was hushed but for the soft music, and the rustle of Rosamund's dress of flame, the slither of their feet on the polished floor.

Scintillas of fiery red from the ring seemed to reach every corner of the room.

It was when they were coming back to the table where Lorna and Mannering were sitting that Mannering noticed a man whom he had not seen before that evening, a man whose presence rang a clanging bell of warning. He had a shapely blonde with him, as colourless compared with Rosamund as a paste gem to a diamond. He was at a table which had not been occupied when Mannering's party had come in; Mannering was quite sure that he would have noticed had the man been there before.

Lorna said, 'What is it, John?' and turned to look in the same direction.

Theo, his arm about Rosamund's waist, came up, looking as if all his fears were forgotten and he was the happiest man alive.

'Tell you later,' Mannering whispered to Lorna as he stood up, and tried not to let the others see how badly he had been jolted.

The man with the shapely blonde was Micky Odell, whom the police were very anxious to catch because he made a fortune out of fooling wealthy men.

He always used a girl to ensnare an old fool.

And Rosamund was 'in his set'.

Chapter Eight

Theo Suggests

'Sure, you can dance with her,' Theo said readily, 'but only once tonight; this is my night. Eh, Lorna?' He stood up and watched as Mannering led Rosamund away for a dance which held a kind of magic. 'Lorna,' repeated Theo, looking down at her, 'will you think it insulting if I ask if we sit this dance out?'

She laughed. 'Of course not.'

'I can imagine that you could be a sensation any time you liked,' Theo said, and clasped Lorna's hand on the table. He squeezed. 'You don't have to tell me how you've kept in the background tonight, I sure do appreciate it. There's something else you can do which I would appreciate even more.' He let her hand go, picked up his glass, and looked over the top of it, into her eyes. Bubbles rose, swift and sparkling.

'What is it now?' asked Lorna.

Theo looked rueful. 'I guess I always ask for too much. Maybe I would have been better off if someone had taken my pants down when I was a kid and tanned the nonsense out of me. But I am what I am and there isn't a thing we can do about it.' His eyes were laughing at her, but she knew that his underlying purpose was serious. 'It's this way,' he went on. 'Rosamund lives in a dump of an apartment, and she lives alone. Oh, it's all right, I guess, but it isn't the kind of place I want my future wife to live in. Also, it's a long way from my hotel, and I have to be central because I'm handling a lot of business while I'm here. I guess I could persuade her to move into the Panorama Hotel, but—' He shrugged and put his head on one side. 'You know how some folk are. If we stay at the same hotel, everyone will assume we're living together, and I don't go for premarital promiscuity. No, ma'am, not with the girl I'm going to marry!' His irrepressible smile sparked up again, to his eyes and to his lips. 'It so happens that Rosamund hasn't any folk, none who matter, anyway. She's lived on her own in London for years. There's an aunt in Scotland and a sister in America, one of the GI brides, and that's the end of it.

'In the next three weeks she'll need someone to talk to, someone who knows her way around. She's going to have quite a job buying her trousseau, so she'll need a lot of help. I guess that's not one of the ways I can chip in! So I was wondering ...' Theo hesitated, sipped his champagne, tried to grin but couldn't quite manage to make it spontaneous. So he clasped Lorna's hand more tightly. 'Do you have a spare room? Could she stay with you? That would be fine and handy to your studio, and maybe if you've time you could help—' He broke off and raised his hands in a gesture of surrender. 'Okay, okay, I'm crazy! There are people you can have your own way with and there are people who have a will of their own. You and John are in the second group. Forget it.'

Lorna studied him contemplatively. The band was playing a foxtrot, and seemed far, far away. She saw the sharp, clear-cut, handsome features, the tanned, healthy skin, the fine, clear, pale blue eyes, the crisp, curly hair, the vitality, the strength, the personality which showed itself even when Theo Wray was sitting like this, quite still, now that he had lowered his arms.

'Wouldn't it be better if you told me what you really mean?' she asked.

'Come again?'

'You really want to make sure that Rosamund isn't alone, and you think John will be able to look after her better than anyone else.'

Theo gave a little explosive sigh. 'You and John make quite a team,' he declared. 'I'm glad I don't have to do big business with you. I like winning. Sure, that's a reason. It's not the only reason, but it's a big one.' His smile was unbelievably frank and open. 'Sure, you know I could fix it with some dowager, one of these society dames who used to prepare girls for presentation at court. I've been inquiring about it – but don't tell Rosamund, she doesn't know! She would say she didn't want to go, but she would go after a while. This way, it would look more natural, and she could have protection without having any idea that she's being protected.'

'You wouldn't make the mistake of thinking that Rosamund is a fool, would you?' Lorna asked.

Theo spread his hands. 'She's not a fool, but she's got simplicity,' he asserted. 'She's so honest that it wouldn't occur to her that the world is not only full of wolves but of bad men too. That's the thing which fascinated me. There's another word—what is it?' He waved his hands, and finished explosively, 'Purity! Know what I mean?'

'I know exactly what you mean,' Lorna said.

Just beyond Theo, still sitting down and facing their way, was Micky Odell. The blonde was drinking and looking about her, a pretty little thing with an upturned nose and shoulders so bare that, from the back, it looked as if she was wearing a topless dress. Odell was striking-looking, dark and pale, with fine eyes and well-marked eyebrows and lashes which gave the eyes an added brilliance. He had a strong mouth and chin too; he was not by any means handsome, but every woman would look at him twice.

He was staring. It was almost impossible to imagine that he was smiling; or sneering. He glanced from them towards the floor, and Rosamund and Mannering were quite close now; obviously he was looking at the girl.

'You seen someone you don't like?' Theo asked, quietly.

'No one who matters.' She went on, 'Yes, I think I'd like that, Theo.'

'You'd like what?'

Lorna laughed at him with her eyes, and didn't speak. Suddenly her meaning dawned on him, his face lit up, he jumped to his feet, rounded the table, gripped her hands, and hugged her; the table rocked when he banged against it; a little champagne spilled.

'Gee, that's wonderful! You don't know how happy you've made me. Happy and relieved. I sure don't want anybody to get at Rosamund. You mean it? Sure, sure, I take that back, you wouldn't say anything you don't mean! But will John agree?'

'You must persuade him,' Lorna said dryly.

'Sure,' said Theo, as if that were a trifle which hardly needed considering. 'Gee, that's wonderful! Listen, Lorna, we've got to fix it tonight. Strike while the iron's hot. It will be half past two or three o'clock before we leave here, and Rosamund will be so tired she won't mind where she sleeps so long as she can get her head down on the pillow. How about suggesting she stays with you for the night? You can find everything she needs. Then you can easily suggest that she stays with you tomorrow – if the suggestion comes from you she'll think it's wonderful. Can do?'

Lorna laughed. 'Can do.'

'Wonderful! Now we're going to dance; who wants to sit out? Can you tango?'

'Yes, but this dance is nearly over.'

'Phooey,' scoffed Theo. 'What's the band there for, if it isn't to please the customers?' He drew her to her feet, and as the last beat of the foxtrot came, reached the bandleader, a tall, lissome, graceful man. 'Can you go into a tango, quick? I've got my reasons,' Theo asked. There was a rustle of paper, and a five-pound note appeared in the bandleader's right hand. 'Tango, right?' repeated Theo. 'Now, one, two, three ...'

'Oh, I'd love to stay just for the night,' Rosamund said, and her eyes lit up, although already she was looking very tired. 'My apartment will be so dull, after this.'

Theo winked at Lorna.

They weren't likely to stay as late as half past two, Lorna thought. It was now after one. Rosamund sipped champagne, but had to stifle a yawn. The excitement had been heady, the champagne more heady still, and she would probably sleep the clock round. She seemed content to sit a dance out for the first time during the evening, and Theo was beating time with his foot and with a fork against a glass, for they had taken supper so that they could also take a drink.

Mannering had seen the way Odell kept glancing towards the table, but Theo's head and shoulders hid Odell from the girl, so there was no way of being sure that she had seen him.

She tapped her mouth with the tips of her fingers, trying to stifle a yawn, and Theo looked as though he did not know the meaning of tiredness.

'Care to dance, honey?' he asked.

'No, I'd rather not,' Rosamund said. 'I'd rather—' She broke off, staring beyond Theo, staring at Micky Odell, who had risen to his feet and was now looking straight at her. He had that curious, sneery little smile at his lips. The blonde was getting up too, and if she noticed that her escort was not really interested in her, she did not appear to mind. She just stood, waiting.

Theo turned round, as if worked by clockwork.

He and Micky Odell stared at each other, and Mannering could see the almost derisive look on Odell's face, although he could not see Theo's. He did, a moment later. Odell took his partner on to the floor, and Theo turned back to the table, frowning, his eyes harder than they had been since Mannering had challenged him about the incident in the street.

'That someone you know?' Theo asked abruptly.

'I've met him,' Rosamund answered.

Theo swung round on Lorna. 'That the guy you were staring at, the guy you didn't like?'

Lorna didn't answer, but glanced at Mannering.

'Theo—' Mannering began.

'It's the same guy,' Theo said, and his voice was hard and clipped. 'And he scared you, Rosamund. I can see when you're scared. Who is he?' When no one answered, he went on almost harshly, 'Don't hold out on me. Who is he? If he or anyone else harms Rosamund, I'll kill him. The quicker he knows it the better.' He began to get out of his chair.

Chapter Nine

Clash

Mannering said sharply, 'Sit down.'

Theo continued to rise to his feet, staring at the tall figure of Micky Odell. The shape of the blonde seemed to have changed, and had taken on the contours of Odell's figure, so closely did she press against him.

'Sit down,' Mannering said. 'If you don't, I'm through with you.'

Theo, standing upright, turned to stare at Mannering. Rosamund looked as if she couldn't be sure what was in his mind, and as if she was seeing something in him which she could never understand.

But she had been scared when she had seen and recognised Micky Odell.

Lorna was quite sure of that; and Theo had been sure.

'Theo, sit down,' Mannering said, more lightly, 'and repress the primitive in you.'

It would take more than words to do that; he felt quite sure that Theo was living on his nerves, and had been for a long time. If he got much worse, he would probably have a breakdown. His remarkable gift of concentration kept him going, but all the signs of a man subjected to severe nervous strain were there.

Theo probably didn't realise it, but what he needed were three months of complete rest.

He was angry enough now to pick a quarrel with Micky Odell. Yet a logical explanation would calm him, provided it explained why

Rosamund had looked so alarmed. Mannering knew of none, so he invented one, swiftly. 'That's an old boy friend of Rosamund's. She was startled when she saw him here.'

'Boy friend?' Theo's voice was clipped. 'She didn't tell me that she had any boy friend.'

'Sit down and be your age,' Mannering said sharply. 'You may have lived like a eunuch for the whole of your life, but normal people do normal things. They eat, drink, laugh, dance. Boy meets girl, they have fun, they part company. Just get your mind out of those cyphers, and remember the flesh and the blood.'

'Oh,' said Theo, and gave a little, almost sheepish, grin. 'Sure, I just got mad.' He sat down. 'I got mad because I don't want anyone to have anything to do with Rosamund, and if anyone harms her—'

'We've heard you once,' Mannering said. 'You're talking out of the back of your neck.'

'Hey, John! You mind what you're saying.'

'I'm saying that if you're not careful you'll behave like a man from the outback, a man from the sticks, a primitive,' Mannering said. 'You're living in a civilised world and a civilised society. You can't always have your own way, and it's time you stopped trying to.'

Theo was going very white about the mouth, and there was a cold light in his eyes. 'That's plenty, from you or anyone else.'

'I hope it is,' said Mannering, and his voice was as cold as the expression in Theo's eyes.

The band was playing. Most of the people left were dancing. Waiters stood about idly, several of them very interested in the sudden change of mood at Mannering's table. Rosamund clutched Lorna's hand, as if she wanted more than moral support. Her lips moved, and Lorna just caught the words, 'Don't let them quarrel.'

'Maybe you and I aren't going to get along so well as I hoped we would,' Theo said, very softly. 'I guess we'd better part company before we run into real trouble.'

'What on earth's the matter with you two?' Lorna demanded, although she knew quite well why Mannering had reacted so sharply. In the face of another outburst he would react just as sharply again, or Theo would become dominant. 'I think we're all tired. Rosamund's coming home with us, and I'm not going to allow a silly quarrel to prevent that. Shall we go now, John? It won't take Rosamund and me five minutes to get our things.'

'Why not?' Mannering said. 'You go ahead, while I pay the bill.'

'I pay the bill,' Theo said arrogantly.

Mannering stood up as Lorna and Rosamund got up, and Rosamund looked straight ahead of her, as if afraid to look into Theo's eyes. Odell was at the other side of the dance floor, looking their way; he still seemed to be amused, the girl still moulded herself against him. Theo was standing as stiff as a ramrod. A waiter came, to shift the chairs back.

'Bring the bill, please,' Mannering said, and then relaxed, smiled, and drew a coin from his pocket. Theo was glaring. 'Heads you pay, tails I pay,' Mannering said. 'Or would you rather call?'

There was a moment's pause.

Then: 'You spin, I'll call.' Theo watched the two-shilling piece go up, catching the light. 'Heads.' It came down heads on the back of Mannering's hand, and Theo's eyes lit up. 'I pay,' he repeated. 'In any case it would be crazy to have you pay for this night of all nights. What got into you, John? That the way you always treat your friends?'

'I can't afford to be mixed up in a fracas here, nor can you,' said Mannering, sitting down again and taking out cigarettes. He had already learned not to offer them to Theo. 'Did anyone ever tell you that even a human dynamo gets run down, and that you're overdoing it? Any more outbursts like that will scare Rosamund much more than any old flame will.'

'You didn't see the look in her eyes. She was scared.'

'If you saw a scratch on her chin you'd think it done with a carving knife,' Mannering said. 'You're not seeing things straight, because you're living too much on your nerves. Sooner or later you'll have to give them a rest.'

'I'm going to give them a long rest on my honeymoon,' Theo announced, and seemed to be completely himself again. 'But I don't like the look of that guy. How long was he a friend of Rosamund?'

'I don't know.'

'How much do you know about what you do know?'

'Sometimes not much. I've seen Rosamund at dinner dances and night clubs with the chap over there, and, judging from the way he looked at you, he'd like to break your neck. Rosamund is quite a prize, in case you didn't realise it. I don't want you in a magistrate's court tomorrow morning charged with assault and battery, and I don't want him there, either. If I were you, I wouldn't try to make Rosamund talk too much about this. If it's upset her, she'll take a while to get over it. Forget it for tonight, anyhow. Tomorrow she'll probably feel she can talk freely about it.' Mannering motioned the waiter away, although the man held the bill. 'Knowing you, and seeing how you can flare up like a volcano, she probably thought it wiser not to say anything about the fact that she's had other boy friends.'

Theo was now smiling contentedly. 'It happened once in Australia and twice in America,' he said, apparently apropos of nothing. 'Meeting guys who made me enjoy the fight, I mean. Guys like you. Okay, John. If it comes to that,' he went on with the devastating honesty which seemed an integral part of his character, 'I wouldn't like Rosamund to know how much of a man I've been with some of the damsels who thought that it would be pleasant to be on my payroll. Okay, let me pay that bill. I won't say a word to Rosamund about all this.' He glanced at the bill, put down notes to cover it and a good but not overgenerous tip, then moved towards the door. He glanced at the dance floor as he moved. Micky Odell was quite near, looking towards him. The girl seemed to have fallen asleep; her movements were like those of someone dancing in a trance. 'But I'd sure like to pick a quarrel with that guy,' he added. 'Do you know who he is?'

'Micky something or other,' said Mannering casually. 'And you keep out of quarrels; you've got a marriage on your hands.'

'I'd just like one poke at him,' said Theo longingly. Mannering wondered what would happen if Theo ever learned who Micky Odell really was: what he would do if he was told that some people believed that Rosamund was part of a plot to fleece him. Was she?

The women came as soon as Mannering and Theo reached the foyer. This time the cloakroom girl found time to glance at Mannering and at Theo, and seemed undecided about who warranted attention more. The doorman was waiting, as if he had already been warned to expect them. The Bentley was only a few yards away, and they could walk towards it; there was no need for Theo to fetch it.

'Goodnight, sir, goodnight, Madam. Mr Mannering, sir, could you spare me a moment?' The doorman knew Mannering of old, and might want any kind of favour.

'You carry on,' Mannering said to the others, and smiled. 'Yes, Fred?'

'Just thought I'd tell you, sir,' the doorman said in a whisper. 'There's a chap on a motorbike, been hanging around a lot for the past couple of hours. He was behind you and the Bentley when you arrived.'

'You were right,' said Mannering. 'Thanks a lot.' He hurried after the others, for a word with Theo before they started off, then felt a spasm of alarm. A short man stepped out of the shadows towards the Bentley as the party of three reached it. Mannering began to run, and called, 'Look to your right, Theo!'

Theo was already looking to his right.

A street light fell upon the face of the short man, who made no attempt to conceal himself.

'Hi, Charley,' Theo greeted, and Rosamund seemed to echo the greeting with a subdued, 'Hallo, Charley.'

'John, I want you to meet Charley Simpson, who looks after me like a brother,' Theo went on. 'Bodyguard, secretary, masseur, chauffeur, and all the rest rolled into one. Follows me everywhere like Mary's little lamb, unless I manage to dodge him, or give him so much work he has to be in two places at once.'

'Like tonight,' Charley said dryly. 'But you're asking for trouble, and you know it.'

'I can go out by myself sometimes; I'm a big boy now,' Theo said mildly. 'Charley, this is Mr John Mannering. You were finding out all you could about him last night, remember?'

Charley looked up.

He had a strong, frank, open, easy-to-smile face, with a broken nose, a broad forehead, a square chin. There was something familiar about him, but Mannering couldn't place him for the moment, and he didn't comment, just shook hands. Charley's grip was very firm.

'And Mrs Mannering, you know, the portrait painter,' Theo went on, waving his hand at Lorna.

'Glad to know you, Mrs Mannering,' Charley said. 'Proud to meet you, Mr Mannering.' His voice was pleasant, more cultured than Mannering had expected: undoubtedly public school. 'Theo, you ought to be ashamed of yourself, Rosamund looks tired out.'

'This is my night,' Theo said, half ruefully. 'All the world is putting me in my place. You want to know something, Charley? Rosamund's staying with the Mannerings tonight.'

'Why, that's wonderful!' Charley sounded delighted.

'You've said it,' said Theo. 'Why don't you take half a day off and go back to the hotel? I'll be able to get myself from Chelsea to the Panorama.'

'I had my half day off at dinner,' said Charley dryly. 'And old Bettley left at ten o'clock, with plenty for me to do, so the quicker we start, the better.'

'What did I tell you? Everywhere poor Theo went, Charley lamb was sure to go,' misquoted Theo. 'Have it your own way.'

Charley followed them, waited outside as they went up to the flat, and drove after the Bentley when, about two o'clock, Theo drove away. It was as if Charley, much more than Theo, believed that there was cause for fear. Coupled with the incident earlier in the evening, and the fight with the two men from the Jaguar, it was enough to make Mannering wonder what lay behind this fear, and behind the need for Theo's having a constant watchdog. And why did Theo pay a guard, then sometimes take pleasure in avoiding him?

He could worry about all this tomorrow, Mannering decided.

'I don't care what you, Bristow, or even Micky Odell says, she's absolutely and helplessly in love with Theo, and she wouldn't work with anyone against him,' Lorna said, as she entered the main bedroom after leaving Rosamund. 'I don't know why she was scared of Micky Odell, though.'

'You agree that she was.'

'Of course she was. I wouldn't be surprised if he isn't trying to make her work against Theo, but I don't think anything in the world would.' Lorna stifled a yawn. 'I'll start the portrait in the morning, and get her talking. I don't think it will be long before she tells me all about it.'

'If you really did what Theodorus would like, you'd go up to the studio now and start preparing the canvas,' Mannering said.

'If that's funny, I'm too tired to see it,' Lorna said. Then she caught sight of her reflection in the mirror, stared, and said almost sadly, 'Even when I was her age, I wasn't a patch on her, and it's no use telling me that I was.'

'You weren't a patch on her,' agreed Mannering solemnly.

'Don't be a brute,' said Lorna tartly.

Mannering woke first, a little after eight o'clock, saw that Lorna was sleeping very soundly, got out of his bed without disturbing her, and pulled on his dressing gown. Once in the lounge hall, he heard the chink of cups: Claudia was getting ready for the morning tea, and would almost certainly have a kettle singing, so as to make it the moment either of them rang. He went to the kitchen door, and the grey-haired maid looked round, a rather severe-faced sixty-two or -three, with her hair drawn straight back to a bun. She was ultra-efficient but, as far as Mannering knew, not particularly warmhearted. The creed of Claudia might be called: I Know My Place.

'Good morning, sir.'

''Morning, Claudia. Tea for one, please. I won't disturb Mrs Mannering yet.'

'Very good, sir. Will you have it in the study?'

'The dining room. And I'll have breakfast in half an hour,' Mannering said. 'Don't go into the spare room. Miss Morrel stayed the night, and may be staying for a while longer.'

'I won't disturb her or Madam, sir.'

'Fine,' said Mannering, and whistled softly as he bathed, then shaved, crept into the bedroom for his clothes, and found Lorna stirring but sleepy enough to say that she didn't want any tea yet. Dressed, he went out. The post came, but there was nothing of much interest in it, nothing to push Mannering's thoughts off the problems which Theo Wray had caused, and the problem of Rosamund and Micky Odell. Lorna was probably right, and would be able to make the girl talk; once she did, they might be able to find the truth. Running through all his musings was the evidence of taut nerves in Theodorus: in a dangerous surge of overwhelming fury, Wray might do irretrievable harm. Cause for jealousy would probably spark off another outburst.

Mannering was glad when Lorna rang; he went in, and found that she couldn't get to sleep again.

Claudia brought her tea.

'You look disgustingly fresh,' Lorna complained.

'It's my clean living,' Mannering retorted. 'Awake enough to tackle a problem, sweet?'

'If it's not too involved.' In a pink bed jacket, Lorna looked fresh and much younger than she had any right to expect. 'About Rosamund, I suppose, and the boy friend you invented for her last night.'

'Yes.'

'I was never keen on white lies,' Lorna said, sipping her tea, 'and this one could cause a lot more complications than most. I'll talk to her, and telephone you at the shop. Must you be so early there this morning?'

'I think I'm going to need time off during the day,' said Mannering, and kissed her, and left the flat.

As he turned into the street, he saw a parked Vespa, of palest blue, and after that wasn't really surprised to see Quinns' Thomas coming towards him. The oldest of the Tom, Dick, and Harry trio looked refreshingly young, brisk, and capable. He had not distinguished himself at Oxford, from the scholarly angle, scraping through with a pass, but he had been Universities' heavyweight champion for three years.

'Hallo, Tom, still on duty?' Mannering greeted.

'I thought I'd better be, sir.'

'Quite right. Sure it's your cup of tea?'

'One of the reasons I came to Quinns was to be at hand if there was any trouble,' Tom reminded him with an appreciative grin. 'It was John Mannering the investigator rather than John Mannering the collector and connoisseur I wanted to work for. So unless you've someone else in mind, I'd very much like to keep the job of looking after Miss Morrel.' He tried not to show how much this mattered.

Mannering said, 'You've got the job, Tom.'

The glowing brown eyes lit up. 'That's wonderful! Thanks very much.'

'And you're in the right place to start,' said Mannering. 'She's here now. But you'd better go back to Quinns and we'll sort things out there, then you can come back. I doubt if Miss Morrel will be awake for a couple of hours.'

'I'll go ahead, and clear the way for you,' promised Thomas.

There was a heavy mail at the shop, and Thomas was dealing with several current inquiries; he had to pass on technical details to Larraby. The shop was blessedly quiet, and only two people came in before half past ten. By then, Mannering had cleared his desk, and was ready to send Thomas back to Green Street. His hand was actually on the bell-push to summon him when the telephone bell rang: the line direct to his desk, with a number known to few.

He lifted it.

'Mannering here.'

'John.' It was a breathless Lorna: if he were right, a nervous one. 'I'm worried out of my wits. Rosamund got up just after you left, and seemed as happy as she could be, until she had a telephone call.'

'A call for her?'

'Yes. A man whose voice I didn't recognise asked for her. I've never seen such a transformation. She lost her colour so quickly I thought she was going to faint. She hardly said a word, just: "All right, I'll come," and then put the receiver down. I didn't question her at the time – it would have been useless – but I thought I'd have time to over breakfast. She didn't have anything to eat, though, just went and got dressed. I'd lent her a morning frock which was rather too large,' Lorna added, talking as if she was really worried. 'Then she said she had to go out, she was sorry she couldn't say where, and went off, looking really ill. I tried to persuade her to tell me what was the matter, but she wouldn't say a word. Then I looked out of the window, and—John, Micky Odell was waiting for her in a car.'

Chapter Ten

Pressure

Rosamund saw Odell as she stepped out of the house, and she hesitated for a moment, looking almost as if she would turn round and run up the stairs again. But she did not. Odell stood by the side of a low-built Italian sports car, its pale blue shining in the morning sun. He smiled at her, and there was the slightly sneery look on his face which had been there the night before. He opened the door for her, and Rosamund hesitated again, then stepped in. He closed the door with exaggerated care, and, without saying a word, climbed in the other side. He switched on the ignition, started the engine, and eased the car away from the kerb.

He drove to the Embankment, and then along towards the centre of London, but he soon turned off, and headed for the dense mass of houses beyond.

Rosamund felt the turmoil of her thoughts mingling with fear of this man. Her heart was pounding. She longed for him to speak, and yet hated what she was sure he was going to say. But although he kept silent, and was obviously waiting for her to speak, she said nothing. Now and again he glanced at her.

She didn't look at him, just sat with her hands in her lap, wearing her own evening gloves and Lorna Mannering's dark blue dress, which was a little full at the breast and the waist, as well as an inch or so too long.

At last Odell spoke, with an edge to his voice. 'If you think you can outsmart me, pet, you've another think coming. Don't forget that.'

'I'm not outsmarting you or anyone,' Rosamund said tensely. 'I told you a week ago that I wouldn't have anything to do with defrauding anyone, and the last person in the world I'd let you cheat would be Theo.'

'And I told you that you'd find yourself in a lot of trouble if you didn't do what I told you.'

'I don't care what you say,' Rosamund said. 'I'm not going to help you, and if you attempt to cheat Theo, I shall tell him what you're trying to do.'

She was looking at him now, and saw the way he smiled, the corner of his lip curling, so that she could just see his white teeth. There had been a time when she had thought him wonderful; nearly all the girls who moved into his set did. He could be wonderful too. He could behave as the kindest, most generous man alive, and his gentleness was unbelievable.

He could hurt, also.

And he could frighten.

She had told herself that she was free from him; that although she had friends who were not free and still worked with him, she could stay within that set, yet not be compelled to do whatever he wanted. She had not realised how clever he was.

She was beginning to.

He drove with a light, almost delicate touch, and the car weaved in and out of the traffic, outpacing every other vehicle but seldom appearing to go very fast. People stared; no doubt many with envy. They reached Kensington High Street, not far from Rosamund's apartment, and she realised that he was taking her there.

The traffic thinned.

'I don't want to be unreasonable, Rosie,' he said, using the diminutive which she had outgrown years ago. 'I don't want to break up your plans for the future. If you're in love with Wray, that's all right with me – marry him, set up house with him, whether it's on board a yacht in the Mediterranean or a villa in the Bahamas. I don't want to get in anybody's way. But he's got a lot of money – he has so much that it hurts even to think of it – and I want a share. Not just that ring you had last night, but a good share. That's all.'

'I told you last week that I couldn't help you.'

'*I'm* reminding *you*, *you're* not reminding *me* of anything,' Odell said. He moved his lips very little as he spoke, and consequently had a quiet voice, but it was not really soft. 'I want some of Wray's money. If I took half of it, you would never know the difference. He could still smother you in mink and sable, diamonds and pearls; he could even build you a house with uranium, or let you have crude oil in your swimming pool. Money doesn't mean anything to Theo Wray, but it's a dream to me. It was my lucky day when he went to see Norm Kilham. You don't know how lucky! Know what, Rosie? I can retire after Theo has given me a generous share, and I'd like to retire. Maybe we could have next-door villas in the South of France.'

'I've come today for one reason only,' Rosamund said. 'To make you understand that there is nothing you can do to make me help you. Nothing at all.' Her voice seemed thin and almost squeaky, and she was still afraid, for there was one way in which he could bring pressure upon her: a way which might prove unbearable.

He turned into the street where she lived and pulled into the kerb, but he didn't get out. He put a hand on her knee; his fingers hurt her.

'You've got it wrong, Rosie,' he said. 'I *can* make you. I don't want to have to use unpleasant persuasion; I don't want trouble of any kind. All my life I've been getting rich without making trouble for myself, but when a prize like this one is dangled in front of my nose, I'll take a little more risk than usual. Not that it's a risk, if you do what I tell you to. Any man who will give you a ring which is worth the better part of a hundred thousand pounds will give you the world. All you have to do is to get a passion for jewels, honey. Just get an all devouring passion for the beauties, and let Theo buy them simply to see the light in your eyes. He could make you a gown of diamonds and underclothes of spun gold and shoes of platinum, and still wouldn't have spent more than petty cash. So all you have to do is to get yourself loaded with jewels, Rosie. I'll arrange to have them stolen from you, see? You don't have to do a thing; you're just the sweet, simple little woman who was waylaid and robbed.'

Rosamund began to open the door of the car. 'I won't have anything to do with it,' she insisted. 'If I see Chloe or Frances or any of your favourites trying to win his confidence, I shall warn him.'

'You won't, you know,' said Odell, and he put a hand very tightly on her arm, to prevent her from opening the door. 'You won't warn him, because if you do, it will tell him one or two things that might upset your applecart. Do you think he would be so pleased with his dewy-eyed Rosie if he knew all I know about you?'

'I'll have to take that chance.' Rosamund was very thin-voiced, and still frightened, but she meant to open the door and leave him.

His grip was very strong; although she tugged against him, she was unable to get away. 'You aren't going to take any chance, Rosie.' He seemed to speak without opening his lips. 'I've planned this very carefully indeed. And let me tell you something. I'm a married man now; I've got responsibilities. I wouldn't mind retiring, and you're going to help me. I arranged for you to go to that cocktail party because I was told that he might fall for the high neck and the innocent look. You've got me to thank for a lot of things. Your memory is too short, Rosie. Only a few years ago you persuaded a nice old boy—that's your own description, remember?—to make you some very substantial presents. Then you walked out on him.'

Rosamund was very pale. 'You forced me to.'

'You say I forced you to,' Odell sneered. 'Who'd believe that, Rosie? You wanted to protect your kid sister who was in big money trouble, so you did what I suggested – I didn't make you. And you couldn't even prove I suggested it. You got your cut and your sister's a nice girl now, married and in America, where everyone's rich. But you're not in America; you're here. And your boy friend wouldn't shower jewels on you if he knew you'd stuck an old man in exactly the same way, would he? He'd more likely break your neck.'

Rosamund said tautly, 'I'd have to take that chance.'

'Don't do it, Rosie. That old geezer you got the jewels from was one of the few who've ever been really awkward, so I had to buy him off. I liked you, Rosie, and I didn't worry about losing all my profit, even for your sister. And you were very grateful at the time, remember. The old geezer is still hale and hearty, and with a little persuasion he would remember all about it. I'm quite sure he would identify you.'

Rosamund had lost all her colour. 'That was over five years ago. I was too young to realise what you were making me do.'

'Don't keep on,' urged Odell in a harder voice. 'Stop fighting, Rosie, and it will be better for all of us. You'd never persuade a man like Theo Wray to believe that you were as sweetly innocent as all that. Oh, I know you were, but that's not the point. You swindled the nice old boy. You actually cheated him out of money and jewels. It was a few years ago, but the police are always boasting about their long, long arm. Even if your Theo would forget all about it, which he wouldn't, the police would put you away for a year or two. Now stop fighting. The job needn't take long. Properly handled, Theo will never know what happened, and you'll be the last person he'd suspect. I'll come up to your flat with you now, and we'll go into details.'

Rosamund said in a quivering voice, 'If the past has to come out, I can't help it. I'm not going to help you. If Theo is swindled, I shall tell him all I can about you. Now let me go.'

Instead, Odell tightened his grip, and twisted her arm. In front of them was a milkman, carrying a metal basket filled with milk bottles. The milk looked very white in the sun. A post-office van, as scarlet as Rosamund's dress the night before, was at the far end of the street. They saw no one else.

Rosamund gasped in pain.

'Now think again, Rosie,' Odell urged. 'And see it my way, because if you don't, you'll get hurt much more than this. You'll get so badly hurt that—'

He broke off, with a sharp exclamation.

He let her go, and snatched at the ignition key. Rosamund saw him stare in the mirror as if suddenly terrified. She saw him stab the self-starter, and heard the engine roar, but before he could take off the brake, the door was wrenched open and a pair of hands clutched Odel's right arm.

Rosamund saw Odell trying to get his right hand into his jacket pocket. Before he succeeded, he was jerked out of the car as if by irresistible power. Then Rosamund saw Theo. The whiteness around his mouth and the whiteness at his nostrils was bad, but far worse was the hatred in his eyes, and the glittering expression which cried that he could kill.

'Theo!' she managed to gasp, and slid across the front of the car to get out on the same side. 'Theo!' She saw the flurry of legs, heard a gasping sound, and saw Micky Odell stagger backwards, but Theo still held him with one hand, and was striking at him with the other. 'Theo, let him go!' she almost sobbed, and tried to pull him off, because she was so afraid.

She hadn't the strength.

Then a car came speeding along towards them, and she looked up, saw the car stopping, and saw Mannering opening its door.

Chapter Eleven

The Man Who Wanted To Kill

Mannering was out of his car before the door was wide open, and he jumped towards the two men who were struggling by the side of the Italian car. He saw the dread in the girl's eyes, and knew it was justified; in this mood, Theo Wray was a killer. Micky Odell looked as if he was already half conscious; his efforts to defend himself were pathetically weak, and when he kicked out, he lost his balance. Theo kept him upright, then shifted his grip from the lapel to the throat.

'That's plenty, Theo,' Mannering said, but did not think the other heard him. He gripped Theo's right wrist.

For a moment Theo was baffled: then he glanced round, saw who it was, and growled through his set white lips, 'Get out of my way.'

Only force would stop him.

Mannering changed his grip, and twisted. Theo gave a little grunt of pain and surprise. His hold on Micky Odell's throat slackened, so that Odell sagged away. It was Rosamund who saved him from falling, and helped him towards the car, where he leaned against the wing. He looked like a boxer who had been bashed and battered into a knockout. His eyes were glazed, he was gasping for breath, and there were spots of blood at his cheeks, his collar, and his tie.

Mannering hardly noticed that.

He had let Theo go, and the younger man swung round on him, eyes glittering, no longer a killer but furiously angry and set on hurting. 'I warned you,' he rasped, and launched himself at Mannering.

Mannering took one blow on the chest, low down. Then his arms weaved, and he gripped Theo again. There was a moment when they seemed to be standing absolutely still: then Theo began to bend downwards, pushed by an inexorable pressure which Mannering did not relax. Sweat stood out in little beads on Mannering's forehead; the effort was taking a lot out of him. If this trial of strength lasted much longer he might have to give way, and forever after Theo would want to deal with him as he would have dealt with Odell.

He exerted more pressure, clenching his teeth, and seeing that Theo was in just as bad a way.

Then Theo's resistance collapsed, and he thumped to the pavement.

Mannering backed away hastily, quite prepared for the other to spring at him. But Theo crouched on the ground, only looking up, tie pulled out and collar awry, but otherwise untouched. Then he took a phial from his pocket, shook a tablet on to his hand, tossed it into his mouth, and swallowed it.

The whiteness round his mouth faded, and the tension at the nostrils relaxed also. So he was taking drugs – some kind of tranquilliser, probably.

Theo glanced towards the car, and Mannering spared a moment too.

A man whom he had not seen before was helping Odell into the seat next to the driving wheel. Rosamund was standing away from the car. Odell's chin was lolling on his chest, but he was moistening his lips, and once he tried to look round. The other man, who was short and perky and dressed immaculately in grey, didn't say a word, but ran round to the driving seat. He darted a glance at Theo, as if fearful of being the next victim.

Theo said, 'You shouldn't let him go, John,' in a clear voice. 'I wanted to kill him for what he did to Rosamund.'

The milkman, hurrying to see if he could help, heard that and stopped. The driver of the post-office van, who was slowing down, heard it, and looked shaken. A young woman and an old one, one the other side of the road, obviously heard the words before they were cut off by the sound of the Italian car's engine. Without another look round, the driver went off as swiftly as if Theo had been at the wheel; the rear tyres squealed under the fierce acceleration.

Theo said again, 'That was a mistake. I'll have a lot of trouble finding him.' He moved quickly, until he was standing upright. There was no malice, only reproach, in the way he looked at Mannering. Then he stepped to Rosamund's side. 'It's okay, honey,' he went on in the most gentle of voices. 'He won't ever do that to you again; I'll make sure of it.'

The milkman said, 'You'd better mind what you're saying.'

The postman said, 'Well, here's one for the book,' and looked along the street and beckoned. Mannering glanced over his shoulder, and wasn't surprised to see a police constable approaching. The sports car reached the far end of the street, and went out of sight.

Theo had his arm round Rosamund's shoulders. 'Don't look that way, honey. There isn't a thing so bad as you think it is.'

'You'd better go to the flat,' Mannering said. 'I'll deal with the policeman.'

'The who?' Theo glanced along the street, then grinned, as if nothing at all unusual had happened. He ran a hand over his hair, and went on, 'Oh, the copper. I'm told you've got Scotland Yard eating out of your hand, so it shouldn't be difficult to put a nosebag on this chap.' He helped Rosamund towards the door of the house, watched by a dozen people, and by others at the windows of nearby houses. As he went into the house, there was a murmur of conversation and condemnation.

'If you hadn't come along, sir,' the milkman said to Mannering, 'I reckon he'd have killed him.'

'What's all this, Horace?' the policeman asked. He was a comfortable figure and a comforting-looking man, who gave the impression that nothing would ever make him lose his equanimity. 'Going to murder someone?'

'If it hadn't been for this gentleman ...' Horace began. It was ten minutes before Mannering was able to leave them, with the policeman satisfied that there was no cause to make a charge. The front door of the house was open, and Mannering went slowly up the narrow stairs. It had been an ugly interlude, but not really surprising. He had been lucky in one way: he had wanted to see Rosamund quickly, and this had seemed the most likely place. Micky Odell would hardly have taken her to his West End apartment.

Mannering had saved Odell's life, but wasn't likely to get much thanks for it. He might get some from Theo later, and he had learned one fact of great interest. Theo certainly took tranquillising drugs. Some doctors said they were harmless, as many opposed them, and it mattered little either way. At least Theo recognised the need for some kind of cure for his rages.

Rosamund had looked lost and forlorn as she had turned away, Mannering remembered. What pressure could Odell have exerted to make her leave the Green Street flat with him?

Had she explained to Theo?

Theo opened the door just before Mannering rang the bell, stood aside for him to enter, and said, 'It's about time you showed up; I hope you can do something with her.' Then he seemed to realise that he hadn't given the happiest of welcomes, and gave a rueful kind of smile. 'John, I guess when I've calmed down I'll know how much I owe you. There are times when it scares me, I see so red. I saw a doctor who gave me some tablets which calm me down a bit. It's only temporary – guess I need a rest, like you said, and I'll soon be having one.'

'It's absolute madness!' Rosamund declared. She came in from a small room on the left, carrying a tea tray, and looking more composed, although very pale; her eyes had the telltale sign of tears. 'You can't go about trying to kill people who happen to have displeased you.'

'Any man who lays a hand on you—' Theo began.

'Don't be such a fool,' Rosamund said roundly, while Mannering silently applauded, and at the same time realised that she had reached some kind of decision. 'What's the use of making millions of pounds if you're going to spend the rest of your life in prison?' she demanded. 'Money isn't going to buy you off murder in this country or anywhere else. You ought to be kept on a chain while you behave like this. And drugs won't help you. You want rest.'

'Hear, hear,' murmured Mannering.

Theo was strangely subdued as he said, 'You see what I mean; I can't do a thing with her.' He watched as she began to pour out tea, her hand trembling a little, an indication that she was having to fight hard to maintain her composure. Her movements in the everyday job were unstudied and graceful, and when she had finished pouring out, she sat on the arm of a chair and looked at Theo with a severity which drove every other expression from her eyes.

'Mr Mannering, I refused to tell Theo anything until you were here. After the way he behaved this morning, and last night, I don't think I can trust him. But I've made up my mind to tell him exactly why Micky Odell thought that he could compel me to do what he wanted. If Theo then wants to strangle me, will you please restrain him?'

'He doesn't know it, but I've a gun in my pocket,' Mannering declared.

'I can believe it,' said Theo wryly. 'You have everything, including judo. But next time I'll be ready for you. Okay, honey, let's hear this dark secret. Don't say you're a secret drinker, or a poisoner.'

'This—is—not—funny!' Rosamund stormed at him, and so betrayed her tension. She put her tea down untouched, and tears were close to her eyes. 'No, don't touch me. I want to tell you exactly what happened. It was a few years ago. I was not quite eighteen, I'd lived most of my life in the country, and I didn't know my way about. When I was introduced to Micky Odell, I thought he was a kind of dream hero. For a while he couldn't have been more friendly; he wasn't unpleasant in any way at all. But one day …'

She told the story simply; of her sister's involvement with a bad set, and heavy debts. Because of the simplicity, the telling was remarkably vivid. She watched Theo most of the time, but now and again looked at Mannering, as if she found more comfort there. It was impossible even to guess what was passing through the other's mind.

When she had nearly done, she faltered; she was telling of Odell's threat while they had been outside in the car. It dawned upon Mannering that he had not thought of questioning her story; but had taken it as gospel.

Few people were likely to doubt her.

Would Theo?

Would their love break upon this rock?

Theo stood quite still, his face rocklike, his expression quite inscrutable. He was pale, but not white about the gills. His hands were clenched, but not tightly. He was breathing heavily through his nostrils; and that made the only sound except Rosamund's quiet voice.

She said, half closing her eyes, 'And then you came.'

The silence which followed seemed to last so long that Mannering wanted to break it; soon he would have to. It was a silence between these two, and he was not really involved, but he must try to answer the girl's unspoken plea: to be believed, to be trusted, to be loved.

Then Theodorus Wray spoke in a strangely remote voice, stood up slowly, and went towards her, as if in veneration. 'So men come that bad,' he said. 'They'll sink as low as that to make their money.' He stood in front of her, and took her hands. 'Honey, I just want to thank you for the way you told me that story. An hour ago I didn't think there was another thing that could make me love you more than I did then, but I was wrong, I just have one worry. This Odell shouldn't be allowed to get away with it.'

'Forget him, darling; don't think of him anymore. He doesn't matter, now that you know. He just doesn't matter.'

Theo smiled, very gently. 'I guess you're right,' he said, and kissed, then hugged her, and looked over her head at the window. 'I guess we'll forget him,' he went on, but the expression in his eyes told Mannering that it was the last thing he intended to do.

Chapter Twelve

'Forgotten Man'?

Five minutes afterwards, Rosamund began to collect the cups, and noticed that Theo hadn't touched his tea, then found out that she hadn't touched hers. She gave a high-pitched laugh, and a cup and saucer rattled in her hand.

'I'll go and make some more.'

'We don't want any tea, honey.'

'Well, I want a cup if you don't,' Rosamund said, and hurried out; the tray seemed to be banged down on the draining board very heavily.

Theo was smiling, in a remote kind of way. 'She's some girl,' he said with feeling. 'She's got just everything. John,' he went on, more briskly, 'I guess it's time I tried to say real thanks to you.'

'Forget it.'

'If I ever forget it, I'll consider myself on a level with Mr Micky Odell,' said Theo, and his eyes narrowed and that calculating look came into them again. 'From that time on, you can forget me. Okay, we don't talk about Odell. Did Lorna make any arrangements with Rosamund to stay at your apartment for the next week or so? I don't want to talk to her as if I know about that in advance.'

'I doubt if she had time,' Mannering said, 'but leave it to me.'

'Right, thanks. I'm beginning to realise that relying on you is a safe way to live. Now we can talk about Odell. You spun me a yarn last night and I believed it, and maybe it was a good thing I didn't smash his face in when we were on the dance floor, although I would have enjoyed seeing the look in that bandleader's eye. Did you notice the way the guy crimped his hair?' Theo wasn't interested in the bandleader, only in marshalling his thoughts – or his way of approach. He decided on a frontal attack. 'Did you know this Odell was a bad hat?'

'Yes.'

'How bad?'

'He's worked the same kind of trick hundreds of times. He's always used young girls – sometimes bribing them, sometimes having some hold over them. The men involved seldom complain.'

Theo was moving up and down on his toes a little. 'That the limit?'

'That's the limit.'

'No call-girl stuff, and none of this'—he waved a hand disdainfully—'girls hanging about on street corners in the West End? He doesn't run that?'

'He doesn't organise prostitution, doesn't peddle dope, and doesn't ask for the sacrifice which used to be worse than death,' Mannering asserted solemnly.

That won the expected chuckle.

'You keep right on like that and I'll be hearing what a nice guy Odell is,' he said. 'Why don't the police pick him up?'

'He's managed to keep on the right side of the law so far. Whenever there's been a threat of trouble, he's seen that the jewels or the money are returned, and of course he always blames the girls. He's always all right.'

'That guy really wants a lesson,' said Theo.

'One day he'll get all the lesson he needs, and it isn't to come from you,' said Mannering. 'Theo, I don't think you ought to take drugs.'

'They're hardly drugs at all,' Theo said. 'The effect soon wears off. Don't nag me.' He looked up as Rosamund came into the room, carrying the tray again. She had powdered and made up, and her eyes were very bright; she was more like the girl of last night again.

'Mr Mannering,' she said, 'I just can't thank you enough. I know that's a banal thing to say, but it's true.'

'You can thank me enough,' said Mannering, and Rosamund looked surprised. 'Lorna wants to paint you in the dress you wore last night, and wants to do it soon, because she has some work coming along in a few weeks' time that she won't be able to postpone. And I want to make sure that you're not in trouble from Odell. If you stay here, anything might happen, and before we know where we are, Theo will be accused of murdering him. I want you to come and stay with Lorna and me. Lorna was talking about it at breakfast.'

Rosamund's eyes were now laughing at him. 'You mean Theo was talking, either this morning or last night,' she said. 'I just can't understand how it is he manages to twist everyone round his little finger.' She hesitated, and then went on with her refreshing honesty, 'Yes, I'd love to, if you're sure I won't be in the way. I think I almost hate it here, and to think that I'd someone like Lorna to give me some advice would be wonderful.'

'Perfect,' Theo finished for her.

'Perfect!'

'Then that's fine,' said Mannering. 'I'll let Lorna know right away. How about settling in this afternoon?'

Rosamund said rather unsteadily, 'You're all so good to me. Yes, I'd love to. It won't take long to pack what I must take, and I can come over any time. I—' She broke off, for there was a ring at her front door, and automatically she went towards it.

'I'll go,' said Mannering, and was much too quick for her. He opened the front door, half prepared to believe that Micky Odell had sent an emissary or two to take revenge, and ready to deal with them. Certainly Odell would not take what had happened lying down. But the caller wasn't Micky or anyone like him: it was Charley Simpson, with his ready smile and his stocky strength.

'My boss around?' Charley inquired amiably. 'He told me he would be back by eleven o'clock. I ought to have known better than to let him go out loose.'

Theo called, 'Hi, Charley, come in and have a cuppa.'

Charley came in. He was much sturdier than he looked at first sight; he had fine shoulders, a deep chest, and a springy walk which told of a man at the peak of training.

'Hallo, how are you,' he said to Rosamund. 'Hi, Boss. You've missed one call from Paris, one from Berlin, one from New York, and one from Galveston, Texas. Unless you get back to the Panorama Hotel pretty soon, you're going to be the most unpopular man the switchboard operator ever heard of. I said I'd get you back in an hour, and that leaves forty minutes to go.'

'Okay, okay. I'll come as soon as I can. John, could you handle things here?'

'I'll see that everything's all right,' promised Mannering. 'You go and make another fortune.'

Theo laughed. Charley grinned, and turned towards the door, and it was as he was doing so that Mannering caught sight of the back of his head and the slightly swollen or cauliflower left ear. He exclaimed so sharply that all of them jumped.

'Charley!'

Charley spun round on his heel. 'What the dev—' He broke off when he saw Mannering smiling broadly. 'Well, I don't seem to have done anything I shouldn't. Can I help you?'

'I've just placed you,' Mannering said. 'Southpaw Simpson, isn't that it?'

Rosamund looked puzzled.

'That's it,' agreed Charley happily. 'I couldn't make a living out of being a prize-fighter, and the boss took pity on me.' He gave an infectious grin. 'I'll admit that there are times when I think I ought to take pity on him. He's trying to crowd in three months' work in three weeks, because he wants a long honeymoon, and he crams in two weeks' work in one all the time. Theo, if we don't get back, we'll have Buenos Aires, Sydney, and Calcutta squealing for you at the same time.'

'I'm on my way,' said Theo. He squeezed Rosamund's hands, then sped towards the door and went out as quickly. More sedately, Charley followed; then Charley turned at the door and beckoned.

Mannering went across, and Charley said in a very quiet voice, 'He's not safe running around on his own. If he doesn't run into someone, someone will run into him. He crossed a pretty nasty group of people in Australia, and they don't want him to live until his next birthday, unless he'll agree to do what they want him to. He won't. I've persuaded him to have a secretary at the hotel, and she's a damned good woman, but I have to be there part of the time. I can't keep on his tail as much as I'd like to. And what with his usual working pressure, it's too much for him.'

Theo called from downstairs, 'I thought Mars wanted me, you broken-down prize-fighter!'

'Coming!' Charley was already edging towards the door. 'I'm worried about him. If you can persuade him to see a good doctor instead of the quack he saw a few weeks ago, it would make a lot of difference.'

'Have I got to come and fetch you?'

'I'll try,' said Mannering.

Charley's eyes beamed their gratitude. 'I'll tell you more about things when I get an hour to breathe,' he said. 'I'm coming up!' Charley Southpaw Simpson fled.

Rosamund said very quietly, 'I've known there was something like that from the first. Theo's not always frightened, but he's frightened a lot of the time. And sometimes he's so tired that he almost falls asleep standing up. Then he throws the fatigue off, and seems all right. I really thought that he would kill Odell.'

'We'll soon get things organised,' Mannering promised. 'And the first thing I'll do is to send for Tom, from the shop. Of Tom, Dick, and Harry.' That brought no smile to Rosamund's eyes. 'Tom will lend you a hand with packing, and get a cab to take you to Chelsea. His number-one job is to look after you.'

She said intently, 'Why are you doing all this for us?'

Mannering smiled as he told her the simple truth. 'I hadn't realised that I was doing much. Theo's just willed it on to me.'

'I think meeting you and Lorna was one of the luckiest things in our lives,' Rosamund said. 'I can't help it, though; I'm really scared.

I find myself up in the clouds one moment, and the next wondering whether we'll ever get through the next three weeks.'

'You will,' said Mannering, confidently.

'Watch her all the time,' Mannering ordered Thomas. 'Don't take any chances at all with her, Tom. Odell might decide to have a crack at her in order to get his own back on Theodorus Wray.'

Tom's look said: 'Over my dead body.'

That wasn't surprising: Rosamund could win worship from a man who had seen her only once or twice.

Mannering reached Quinns a little after half past one, and found Larraby deep in conversation with a withered-looking old man who came from Beirut, and who wanted papyrus scrolls, and Sylvester earnest with a Japanese who was examining two fantastically intricate carvings in jade. Mannering spent five minutes with each seeker after precious things, then went into his office. There were a dozen messages, among them two saying that Superintendent Bristow had called. It was possible that Bristow had heard of the encounter in Kensington, possible that he knew that Odell had been at the Signet Club last night. Mannering put a call in for the Yard man, but Bristow was out, and not expected back until the middle of the afternoon.

'He's on that smash-and-grab at Golders Green,' said the detective who answered from his office. 'Wouldn't be surprised if he wanted to see you about that, Mr Mannering. A lot of secondhand jewellery seems to have been stolen, and a lot of jade too. Wouldn't be likely to steal jade unless there was a customer waiting for it, and I think Mr Bristow wondered if you know anyone after jade in London at the moment.'

The little man from the Far East was within ten feet of Mannering.

'If I hear of anyone, I'll call Bristow,' Mannering promised, and rang off. He finished making notes and then pressed a bell and found Dick at the office door, appearing rather like a genie after the rubbing of the lamp. 'Dick, go and get me some sandwiches and some fruit, will you? I've a lot to do and haven't time to go out. And ask Mr Larraby to come in and see me; tell him I won't keep him a moment. Apologise to the gentleman with him, will you?'

'Very good, sir.' Dick went out, quickly, and almost at once Larraby was in the office, with the door ajar behind him, and the man from the Far East within sight. Mannering spoke so that his words carried only as far as Larraby's ear.

'The Yard's looking for a jade collector who might buy on the side.'

'I see,' said Larraby, and did not need to glance round to show that he knew exactly what Mannering meant. 'I'll get all the information I can, sir, before he goes.' He went out, closing the door very softly behind him.

Mannering put jade and the Japanese out of his mind, and sat back, looking at Lorna's portrait of him as a laughing cavalier, and yet hardly seeing it. The face of Micky Odell was in his mind's eye, and he did not like Micky's expression. Against this, he weighed everything that he and the police knew about the man. Odell had always reduced risks to himself to a minimum. He would be viciously angry about being battered, but would not be likely to attempt revenge in person. He would work through others. It was consoling for people to believe that there were no men in Britain who could be hired for such a task, but as foolish as it was untrue. Mannering wouldn't make the mistake, nor would Bristow. The moment Odell recovered, he would thirst for action. The probable attack would be against Rosamund, who would be much easier to hurt than Theodorus Wray.

Mannering found himself thinking of Theo's naive philosophising about being hurt through those whom one loved.

On the one hand, there was violence; on the other, the fact that Micky Odell would not want to take the slightest personal risk. In any case, there was a simple way in which he could take his revenge, a way which would enable him to watch both Theo and Rosamund suffer. If he passed on details of the five-year-old crime to the police, the police would have to take action. Facts were facts and crimes were crimes, and the passing of years did not necessarily make for leniency. In any case, leniency would have to come from judge and jury. If Bristow, one of the most human of policemen, had heard Rosamund's story, he would have felt exactly as had Mannering. But when confronted with the evidence, he would have to charge the girl.

There was another thing to take into account: the cunning of Micky Odell. It would not be difficult to involve Rosamund in more recent crimes. Simple, for instance, to hide stolen jewellery in that little apartment of hers. The wise thing would be to search her apartment before the police could. It might be a waste of time, but wasted time could be a form of insurance.

At least it was something specific to do.

Mannering was surprised at himself again because of his eagerness to help both Theo and the girl. He was absorbed in the need, which seemed to have become a deeply personal issue.

Richard came in with sandwiches fit for a hungry man, brought from a nearby pub. Richard also brought a bottle of beer. Mannering enjoyed the lunch more than he would a six-course meal, relished the beer, half smoked a cigarette, reflected on the fact that Theo did not smoke, and then went out. He took a taxi to the corner of the road where Rosamund lived, and it did not occur to him that there might be the slightest danger. Several people saw him go into the house, but that did not seem to matter: he was going to search without taking any risk, with Rosamund's tacit approval. He walked lightly up the stairs. The door was closed, and he grinned to himself as he took a penknife from his pocket, one which Bristow and every policeman anywhere would have viewed with stern disapproval. Any cracksman, any burglar, would regard it with envy. It was easy even for Mannering to forget that he had once used a cracksman's tools with surprising dexterity. To this day it did not occur to him that he might have any difficulty in forcing the lock of an ordinary door without leaving any trace of forced entry.

Rosamund's door was not likely to be different from the majority of the others.

He opened it in less than thirty seconds, and stepped inside.

Then he stopped with frightening suddenness, and his heart seemed to pause in its beating.

On the couch where he had sat that morning lay the body of a man, a man killed with a knife, a man whose face was badly bruised and battered too.

It was the body of Micky Odell.

Chapter Thirteen

Alarm

Mannering closed the door very softly and moved across to the still figure on the couch. He hardly needed to feel the pulse in the limp warm wrist to be sure that there was no movement. It looked as if Odell had been trying to get up when he had been killed.

The knife was still in the wound; a polished bone handle, looking clean and fresh, was jutting out.

Mannering drew back from the body, then glanced at the door. His fingerprints would be on the handle, but only there; he had learned over the years not to touch any part of a door. He went across, opened the door, and wiped the inside and the outside clean of prints. He had touched nothing else since he had come in this time, and if there were prints anywhere in the flat, they could be explained by his morning visit; fingerprints superimposed on others on the door handle couldn't be. He put on gloves which he had been carrying, locked the door, turned, and stood very still, looking at the body, fleeting thoughts going through his mind, concerned more with consequences than with guilt.

Micky Odell looked quite ordinary in death. His features were slack and his mouth open a little, and the touch of the sinister had gone. At least he would never be able to give evidence against Rosamund to the police. Someone had made sure of that.

Theo?

The telephone bell startled Mannering. He turned his head towards it sharply. It went on ringing. A call for Rosamund? A call, which, if answered, would betray the fact that a man had been here about this time – a little after three o'clock in the afternoon. There were moments of almost startling silence between the ringing bursts. It went on and on. He moved towards it, taking out a handkerchief, and picked up the receiver: his voice sounded gruff, no one was ever likely to identify it as his.

'Yes, hallo.'

He heard Lorna's voice and Lorna was fooled, he could sense the way she hesitated before she said, 'Is Mr Mannering there?'

He found himself looking at the back of Micky Odell's sleek head, and smiling – because this was Lorna, and she wasn't sure that he would answer.

'Hallo, sweet. I haven't lost the voice trick, then.'

'I didn't think—' she began sharply, and then broke off, as if someone else was speaking to her. She soon came back on the line. 'That was Tom. He wants to know if there are any special instructions, but—John, is Theo there?'

Mannering felt his pulse quickly. 'Why should he be?'

'His friend Charley Simpson just rang up to say that he'd slipped out of the Panorama again, and vanished,' Lorna said. 'There are several long distance telephone calls coming, and Charley wants him urgently. Is he there?'

'No.'

'I promised to ring all the places I could, to try to find him,' Lorna said, and there was a frustrated note in her voice. 'I really don't know why we go to so much trouble for him; he—but never mind that! Have you seen him in the past hour?'

'No. Do you know when he left the Panorama?'

'Just about an hour ago,' Lorna said. 'He had a telephone call, pretended that it wasn't important, sent Charley down to settle a query with the porters over some luggage, and vanished. Charley—' Again Lorna broke off, then sounded bewildered. 'We talk as if we've known these people for years!'

'We're going to,' Mannering said dryly.

He heard a car door slam, and knew that it was in this street and close to this house. Another slammed, loudly. He looked towards the door, and spoke very quietly. 'So it was something he didn't want Charley to know about, and he preferred not to be followed. All right, sweet. Now listen to me: Bristow might come round, and you might hear a lot of things you won't like. But remember, you know nothing.'

'John, what's happened?'

There were footsteps on the stairs, of men hurrying, and if Mannering's guess was right, these were policemen and they were coming here.

'You still know nothing,' he said, 'and don't tell anyone – not Tom, not Rosamund – anyone – that you found me here. Let them think you caught me somewhere else, but not at Rosamund's flat.'

'I see,' Lorna said very quietly. 'All right.'

'Pray for me,' said Mannering.

He replaced the receiver very gently, so that there should be no sharp *ting!* as he rang off. The footsteps had reached the top flight of stairs now, and he judged that there were three men. If they came in here and found him with the body, he would find himself in custody, and soon on a charge. He knew that it would take only a minute or two to force that door, even if the police were less expert than he. There was a hope that they hadn't a search warrant, and they wouldn't break in unless they had. He didn't ask himself what had brought them so quickly, or why the timing was so remarkable.

He went into Rosamund's bedroom, where he hadn't been before. It was furnished with heavy Victorian furniture, and had a clean and polished appearance. He hardly noticed this as he went to the window and looked out. This overlooked a yard, but not the distant High Street; fewer people were likely to see him here.

He pushed the window up wide.

He heard a man call, 'Open, in the name of the law.'

So they probably had a warrant.

He opened a drawer in the dressing table. There were some oddments of underclothes and, at one end, a folded silk scarf. He picked this up and twisted it round the lower half of his face. The banging at the door came afresh, and he thought he heard another sound, as if the lock was being picked.

He put a leg out of the window.

There was a sheer drop of sixty feet, one which would kill him if he fell. Immediately below were two window sills which would give a precarious foothold, but he had to reach them first. The nearest drainpipe was too far away to be useful, and no fire escape was in sight. Not far away, a baby in pink sat in a pram looking up at him, and in another yard a woman was hanging out some clothes.

The banging stopped.

They would soon be in.

Mannering swung himself over, and hung at full length, groping with his feet for the window sill below. If he'd judged the distance properly, he could just make it. He didn't touch it. He felt panic rising, because it wouldn't be a moment before the police came into this room, and if they saw him clinging to the window sill, that would be the end of hope of getting away, and he would have made the circumstances seem even more damning.

His right toe touched the sill below. He managed to squint downwards, and saw that he was too far to one side. He brought his left leg closer, then put his weight on his toes and let go of the sill. For a moment, he swayed backwards. There was nothing between him and the ground. There was nothing to clutch but the sill above, and that would give him away. He used every trick of balance that he knew, and made himself sway towards the wall. His body pressed closely against it, like the blonde had pressed against Micky Odell last night. Only last night! He spread his arms, which seemed to help a little. He felt at the mercy of the baby, of the woman hanging out her washing, of a hundred people who might look out of the window at any moment: but the greatest danger came from the police above, and from the hard ground below.

Slowly, painfully, he edged along until one side was against the wall; then he bent down until he was able to grip the top of the ledge above the window below him. He touched it, while standing with all his weight on the window sill. If anyone was in the room beyond, there would be a shout or a scream. There was no sound.

The room was empty, and the window so wide open that he could get in, if he could open it a few more inches. He would be much safer there than trying to get down another storey while a cry of alarm might be raised. He pushed the window down, and was about to climb in when a young woman wearing only a bra and panties came briskly into the room, a dress and some stockings hanging over her arm. She saw him on the instant, and stopped still, her eyes widening, her mouth opening wide, terror leaping in her.

One scream would bring the police.

In a moment, she would scream.

Mannering spoke in a low-pitched voice, muffled through the scarf. 'I won't hurt you. Don't make a sound, and I won't hurt you.' She just stood there, and seemed to have stopped breathing, as if petrified: she didn't move even when he dropped into the room. 'I won't hurt you,' he breathed.

She tried to scream.

He could see the effort; for a moment it was as if the shriek was actually coming from her throat; but there was only a funny little noise, a silly little noise. She couldn't make a sound. She turned as if to run out of the room, but Mannering moved faster, pushed her from the door, and said desperately. 'I won't hurt you; just keep quiet.'

He was near enough to see that terror in her eyes, to know that the moment she was released from the grip of paralysis, she would scream the walls down. He snatched the dress from her arm, flung it over her head and shoulders, grabbed the sleeves and tied them round her neck. She tried to struggle and beat the air with her arms, but he didn't wait any longer, just went out and closed the door: the key was on his side. He turned it. The flat was almost identical with the one above, and he crossed to the window overlooking the High Street, where so many people could see him. Just outside was a drainpipe; he would have been wiser to have come out this way. He thrust the window up. He could be down that pipe in a trice.

He climbed out, gripped it, and began to climb down. If the police in the flat above were looking out, they might see him. One blast of the police whistle would bring disaster.

Chapter Fourteen

Facts To Face

Mannering reached the ground.

He heard no shout, no whistle of alarm, nothing to indicate that he had been seen. He walked briskly towards the gate in the wall at the end of the yard, taking off the scarf as he did so, crumpling it up and holding it in front of his face, rather like a man with toothache. He went into the service alley, turned right, and soon found himself in the street, only fifty yards from the house which he had just left. He glanced round. A crowd of forty or fifty people had already gathered round two police cars which were parked outside the house where Rosamund had lived. Five women were holding prams, two of them pushing them to and fro in a kind of rock-a-bye rhythm while they gaped at the scene of sensation. An ambulance bell sounded, and that told Mannering that the police hadn't lost any time. The police surgeon would soon be here; the Divisional Police would probably call in the Yard too.

Mannering turned towards the High Street.

He knew that his clothes were badly in need of dusting, that there was a tear in one knee, and that the toes and sides of his shoes were scratched, but there was nothing he could do about that yet; he had to brazen it out. He turned left, at the High Street, as the ambulance came swinging round from the right: and Yard cars would come from the right, too. He walked briskly, then saw a taxi crawling on the other side of the road. He waved, the cabby stopped, and four minutes from the time he had reached the yard, Mannering was in a corner of the taxi, heading for Knightsbridge. From there he could get another taxi either to Quinns or to Green Street, and so confuse any trail.

It was strange to feel hunted.

It wouldn't last, of course. At least, it shouldn't.

He kept a spare set of clothes at Quinns, but if he went into the shop like this, Dick and Harry would notice his dishevelment and would wonder what it was all about: and if they were questioned by the police, they might think it worthy of comment. If he went to Green Street, only Lorna, Rosamund, and presumably Tom would see him: and Tom would probably be self-consciously on guard in the street, and would only have a glimpse of Mannering as he stepped out of the taxi.

'I'll go to Green Street,' he decided, when he changed cabs.

There was Tom, opposite the house, looking massive and quite striking. Tom, who had been to and from the Kensington flat at least twice with baggage, who had been bowled over by Rosamund.

Forget it.

Mannering waved to Tom as he paid the taxi off, and then went up to the studio flat in the automatic lift. He let himself into the flat quietly. No one was in the hall. As he closed die door, he heard someone singing; Lorna didn't sing in the bath. The kitchen door was closed. He went into the drawing room, where Lorna was often writing during the afternoon. She wasn't there. He went to the loft ladder, and heard her moving about up in the studio, her refuge in time of stress. He whistled to her softly, and she came hurrying to the loft hatch, looking down, wearing skirt and blouse but no smock.

'Are you all right?'

'Fine. I'm going to change, and I'll be up. Claudia in?'

'No, out shopping.'

'How long's Rosamund been in the bathroom?'

'Only a few minutes,' Lorna said. 'John—'

He waved and disappeared, went to his bedroom and changed swiftly, putting the dusty, damaged suit and the scratched shoes in the wardrobe. He lit a cigarette, and it tasted harsh; this time he needed a cup of tea. The reflection made him smile, but there was a grimness in the smile as he went to the loft ladder. Lorna had been listening for him, and appeared at once.

'Put the kettle on!' Mannering called, and went to join her.

'It's on.' She stood looking at him, tense, obviously worried, yet her eyes as clear as a girl's and her complexion lovely. 'John, nothing's happened to Theo, has it?'

'No,' said Mannering. 'Nothing has happened to Theo, yet. I want a word with Theo, though.'

'What's happened? You make it sound serious.'

Mannering slid an arm round her waist. 'Yes,' he said, 'it's serious. It isn't exactly what we expected either.'

He told her.

After the first shock, Lorna made no comment and gave no exclamation, and they walked across the studio to the gas ring where she would make tea and coffee, and even boil eggs: everything needed was there. On a canvas beneath the great north light was a sketch of Rosamund, one done very quickly, obviously from memory: Mannering found himself looking at it as he finished the story.

'The Yard might wonder if I was the man who scared the girl, but I don't think they'll be able to prove that I was. They may be able to prove that I went to the house, because I didn't try to hide it. They won't believe that I didn't go in.'

'John,' Lorna said, as little spurts of steam came from the kettle, 'you know what's happened, don't you?' The spurts became a billow of steam, and water began to splutter from the spout, so she had to hurry forward: the teapot, with the tea in, was standing handy. The gas went out with a pop, and Lorna continued on as she stood up with the teapot in her hand, 'You've run your head into a noose because of Theo Wray and Rosamund.'

'The noose isn't a very good fit, sweet.'

'I don't think we ought to take this lightly at all,' Lorna said. When her face was in repose, like this, and she was worried, she could look almost sullen: as if anger stirred in her. But there was no anger, only fear. 'From the moment Theo came into the shop he's been able to make you and me do exactly what he wants. We've become hopelessly entangled. If the police find out you were at the flat this afternoon, they're bound to look for you. Even if Bill Bristow knows you wouldn't be involved, he'd have to come for you. John, I think I'm scared.'

'If I were Rosamund or Theo, I'd be much more scared than you.'

'Do you think Theo did it?'

'I'm sure he's capable of doing it just now,' Mannering said. 'I'm a long way from sure that he'd use a knife. He is a two-fist and judo man, unless—'

'Unless you're hopelessly wrong about him, and he's not living on his nerves, but is really a devil. If a man like him were bad, there's nothing he wouldn't do.'

'I'm holding no brief for Theo Wray at the moment,' Mannering assured her. 'I'm just trying to add up the facts. Theo had a telephone call. It was so important to him that he . walked out on Charley, and on calls coming from all over the world. He evaded Charley, so he didn't want to be followed, and didn't intend that anyone should know where he went. And he hated Micky Odell. Don't tell me that you can't hate a man you hardly know,' Mannering went on. 'He hated.'

'But why go to Rosamund's place?'

'We're still only dealing with the facts; we don't know that he did,' Mannering said. 'We simply know that Micky Odell did.' He moved across to the telephone. 'Is this thing switched through?'

'Yes.' Lorna watched him with the now-familiar tension, knowing how much was rushing through his mind, how one thought seemed to conflict with another.

He dialled a number: she watched, and knew that he was dialling Quinns. She poured out tea as he waited, and put a cup near him, on a small table close to the easel.

'Hallo, Josh   Never mind the Jap and the jade for a minute; I've an urgent job for you. Try to find out if Micky Odell told anyone where he was going this afternoon, will you? Don't breathe a word to anyone in the shop; just put the feeler out among the people who might know. Say that Odell quarrelled with some man this morning, and I'm anxious to find out if Odell's planning to get his own back.'

'Very good, sir,' said Larraby without hesitation.

'If you're asked anything by the police or the Press, don't say a word about this call,' said Mannering. 'And, Josh—'

'Yes, sir?'

'Look surprised when you're told that Odell's been murdered,' Mannering said, and even managed to smile as he rang off.

He picked up his tea, sipped, said, 'Ah, that's good,' and smiled up at Lorna; the tea was laced with brandy, just what he needed. He sipped again, then took out cigarettes, and lit up for them both. Lorna hadn't spoken since he had finished telephoning; he didn't like the anxiety which showed in her eyes, but it was going to last until they knew the truth about the murder of Odell, and until it was quite certain that he could not be blamed.

Abruptly Lorna said, 'It's almost certain that Theo did it, isn't it?'

'No. Possible, that's all.'

'Who else would?'

Mannering drew at the cigarette, without speaking.

'Who else would,' repeated Lorna. 'Oh, that poor child downstairs!'

'Yes,' said Mannering, and sipped the tea again. He looked at Lorna through the haze of steam rising from the cup. 'If "poor child" is right. As far as we know, Theo and Odell hadn't met until last night, if you can call last night a meeting. And this morning, Theo told half Kensington that he would gladly see Odell dead. He may have an ungovernable temper, and it may be roused by tiredness, jealousy, or by any sneer about Rosamund, but he's no fool. Whatever else,' Mannering repeated, very thoughtfully, 'Theo is no fool, remember. He told the world and the police this morning that he was in a mood to murder Odell. Would he go and commit that murder so soon afterwards?'

'John,' Lorna said abruptly.

'Yes?'

'He might be subject to fits of madness. If he really can't control his temper any better than he does, he might be mad. He must have an incredibly brilliant brain. If he has been overworking, or if there is a mad streak in him, would it be surprising if he had a kind of blackout, and lost all sense of reason?'

'Oh, no,' agreed Mannering, 'and unless they decide to have a stab at me first, that's exactly how the police will reason. I don't think they'll stab at me yet. They will at Theo, as soon as they can. I'll be surprised if there isn't a call out for him within the hour.'

Lorna said quietly, 'I can see how your mind is working. You think that Theo might have been framed, that someone who saw the quarrel this morning seized a chance. That might be right and it might be wrong, but whichever it is, you mustn't get involved any further. You must leave it to the police.'

Mannering didn't speak.

'John!' Lorna said sharply. 'You mustn't work on this case anymore. I said before, from the moment he stepped into the shop, we've become involved in Theo Wray's troubles. He's quite capable of dragging you down with him, if he does go down. It's a job for the police and the police alone.'

'Yes,' Mannering agreed, as if he didn't like to admit it. 'A job for Scotland Yard. No respecters of persons. No room for sentiment. They'll just drive straight ahead at Theo, and they won't mind whom they hurt in the process. If it's suggested that he's been framed, they'll laugh. Wouldn't you, if you didn't know what we know?'

'I don't care what you say, you're not to have anything more to do with this.'

'My sweet,' said Mannering gently, 'there are two reasons why I must. The first is that the Yard wouldn't believe that I had stepped out – and if they did believe it, would think it was because I was scared and would soon guess why. The second is that Rosamund—' He broke off.

There was a footstep below, quick and light, and then Rosamund called up in a clear, now-untroubled voice, 'I've finished, Lorna. May I come up, or are you busy?'

'No, come up!' Lorna called. 'John is here, and we're having a cup of tea.' She could not have sounded more normal.

There was a creaking sound, as Rosamund stepped on to the ladder, and then a different sound, of the front-door bell ringing. Immediately the creaking stopped. Mannering, who had stepped to the hatch, looked down and saw Rosamund's upturned face, her hair a little wispy from the steam of the bath, her skin as fresh and clear as a child's, without any powder or lipstick.

'I'll go,' she said, and turned and hurried off; there was a short pause, while Mannering and Lorna heard the opening of the door and her 'Good afternoon,' before a man asked, 'Is Mr Mannering in, please?'

There was only one voice like that in all the world: the voice of Superintendent William Bristow.

Chapter Fifteen

Bristow Barks

Mannering started to go down the loft ladder the moment he heard Bristow's voice, and reached the passage below almost as he heard Rosamund say that she wasn't sure, and would find out: Rosamund might be sweet and innocent, but in some ways she was very quick-witted.

Mannering called out, 'Yes, I'm here! Come in, Bill!' He went into the hall as if eager to see Bristow, and smiled at Rosamund, who was wearing a simple linen dress, and looked fresh and scrubbed. Bristow was contemplating her thoughtfully.

'I called you at the Yard, but they said you were out on that smash-and-grab job at Golders Green,' said Mannering.

'We've got the men and the jade, and now we're after a Japanese collector who's somewhere in London,' Bristow replied. In turn, he smiled at Rosamund: he could seem extremely friendly, although the appearance of affability meant nothing. 'Is this Miss Morrel, John?'

'Yes.' Be very wary, Mannering warned himself. 'Rosamund, this is Superintendent William Bristow of New Scotland Yard.' He wondered what her reaction would be. She must feel alarmed, fearing the possibility that Bristow had really come to see her because of some charge which Odell had made. But she managed to look only a little surprised, and her voice was steady as she said, 'How are you, Mr Bristow?'

'I'm well, thank you. Is your fiancé here?'

'Theo?' She looked surprised. 'No, he's not. I haven't seen him since'—there was the slightest of pauses, before she went on a little more quickly—'since this morning.'

'After he saw Odell?'

Bristow was set on turning the conversation the way he wanted it, as obviously determined to try to make sure that Mannering could not give the girl a lead. It was never possible to be sure of what the Yard man was getting at, invariably wise to assume that it wasn't quite what it seemed. His first attack was on Rosamund, even though smoothly delivered; it might switch at any time.

Rosamund didn't try to avoid Bristow's eyes.

'Yes, after he'd met Mr Odell.'

'Come in and have a cup of tea,' Mannering suggested, closing the door behind Bristow. 'Lorna is in.'

'Just a minute, please,' Bristow said, without looking away from Rosamund. 'How well did you know Mr Odell, Miss Morrel?'

Could she understand the significance of the past tense?

Obviously Bristow meant to step up the pressure because she seemed completely unprepared. He could be stopped; but should he be? If he thought that Mannering was trying to head him off, he would probably assume that the girl knew much more than she did. The five-year-old affair with Odell was comparatively insignificant now: the important thing was Odell's murder. It would be far better if her reaction persuaded Bristow that news of it took her completely by surprise.

Mannering heard the creaking on the loft ladder: Lorna was on the way down.

Rosamund still kept her composure. The fact that she had on no make-up emphasised her pallor, but her eyes were quite calm. 'I've known him for several years.'

'Well?'

'Fairly well, at first.'

'What do you call fairly well, and what do you mean by at first?'

Bristow was driving her into a corner, as if he knew that he had only to increase his pressure to make her give way. She must feel sure that the Yard had been told about the story of that 'nice old man'. She glanced at Mannering almost desperately, and over her shoulder at Lorna, who was very near them. Bristow was still smiling, but that didn't alter the fact that his last question had been sharp and hostile.

'Crowding Miss Morrel a bit, aren't you, Bill?' asked Mannering. 'What's the trouble?'

'Leave this to me, please.' That was almost a bark. What was Bristow up to? Breaking the girl down, or trying to force him, Mannering, to interfere? 'Answer my questions, Miss Morrel, please.'

Lorna said easily and with a smile as charming as it could be, 'Of course she will, but we needn't stand in the hall and talk.' She took Rosamund's arm, and led her towards the drawing room quite naturally; she was half a head taller than Rosamund. Bristow looked exasperated; Mannering smiled as if he had no idea what was in Bristow's mind.

'If you're worried about the quarrel this morning, Bill, I can tell you that Theo Wray had some grounds for it. Odell had made himself very unpleasant.'

Bristow barked, 'Unpleasant enough to be murdered?'

Mannering was ready for it: prepared with the gasp of astonishment, the missed step, the hand raised slightly, as if by reflex action. Lorna must have been half prepared. But Rosamund was taken completely by surprise. She turned round, freeing herself from Lorna's grasp. No one could doubt the genuineness of her astonishment.

Bristow watched her very closely.

Mannering began, 'Bill, are you sure—'

'Quiet, please! Miss Morrel, when did you last see Mr Wray?'

'This—this morning.'

'Haven't you seen him since lunch?'

'No.'

'Quite sure?'

'Yes. I'm positive.' Colour was coming back into her cheeks, and Mannering suspected that she was feeling angry about the sharpness of Bristow's question and his hectoring manner: but above everything else there was her fear: that Theo had killed Odell. On the heels of such fear there might come panic.

'Have you spoken to him on the telephone?'

'No. No, but why—'

'Did you know that he meant to kill Odell?'

Here came the panic, storming into her eyes, showing in the way her lips quivered, and in the nervous spasms of her fingers. It couldn't be wondered at: it was probably exactly what Bristow wanted. It would be possible to stop Bristow and to give the girl some relief, but wouldn't it be better to get this over? Lorna seemed to be pleading with Mannering to interrupt, but he didn't speak or move.

Bristow's voice was very sharp. 'Come, Miss Morrel. Did you or didn't you?'

'I—I don't believe he—he killed anyone.'

'I asked you if you knew that he intended to.'

'No, and it isn't true.'

'What exactly do you mean, Miss Morrel? You were there when he made a vicious attack on Odell. And after Mr Mannering had prevented him from committing murder then, you were present when Wray said he would like to kill him.'

'He was angry. He didn't know what he was saying!'

'He knew enough about what he was doing.'

Rosamund looked despairingly at Mannering, and said in a low-pitched voice, 'He told you he wouldn't let himself go like that again, didn't he? He said he wouldn't.' Her voice trailed off.

'Supposing we get back to the questions,' Bristow said brusquely. 'How well did you know Odell? Exactly what did you mean by saying that you were fairly friendly at first?'

Mannering began, 'I can tell you—'

'I'd rather Miss Morrel spoke for herself,' Bristow rasped. He seemed a different man from the friendly trencherman of the previous day's lunch at the Cannon Row pub. But at least he had shown his hand; he had come to question the girl, to break down her resistance: yet he had come alone, so nothing said here could be used in evidence. 'Now, Miss Morrel, if you will answer—'

'Don't say another word,' Mannering advised cheerfully. 'Bill, I've let you go on long enough. Miss Morrel's our guest. As our guest, I'll try to look after her interests. Care to come and sit down and talk this out reasonably?'

To ease the tension he took out his cigarette case, fingering the matte-gold surface. 'Or would you rather go and get a copper with a notebook?'

Bristow the policeman would take umbrage.

Bristow the friend would stay.

After a long pause, Bristow stretched out a hand for the proffered cigarette, and Lorna took the girl into the drawing room. Rosamund seemed to lean heavily against her, as if suffering physically from the shock and from the interrogation. Mannering drew in the smoke, and asked in a very quiet voice, 'Is Odell dead?'

'Of course he is, or I wouldn't have said so.'

'How?'

'Knifed.'

'Doesn't sound like Theodorus Wray.'

'Whether it sounds like him or not I'd like to get my hands on him,' Bristow said aggressively. 'You know that he looked like a killer only this morning.'

'That's a far cry from being one.'

'You dragged him off Odell,' Bristow said, so proving that he had heard the whole story. 'And if that girl knows where he is now, I want to hear.'

'She's been here all the time since the shindy in the street. I sent young Thomas from the shop to help her back, and see her here. She arrived in time for lunch, and hasn't left the flat.'

'Never heard of telephones?'

'You're being a bit cantankerous, aren't you?' Mannering said. 'If he'd telephoned, Lorna would have told me. I want to see him myself.'

'Why?'

'His right-hand man wanted to find him, and has been trying to get him everywhere.'

'Simpson, you mean,' Bristow said, and sounded mollified: so far he had not given any hint that he had reason to think Mannering had been at the girl's flat that afternoon, but he was capable of keeping that shot in his locker, and firing it when he judged Mannering's defences were weakest. 'Yes, Simpson told me that. I've just come from the Panorama Hotel. Wray left there about two-twenty. Odell was killed somewhere between two and three o'clock, as far as we can judge. The body was quite warm when we found it.'

'Where did you find it?' Mannering asked innocently.

'At Rosamund Morrel's flat.'

'Good God!'

Bristow looked at Mannering broodingly, as if he wasn't sure whether to be impressed by that vehemence or not. At least he was giving Rosamund time to recover her composure. Probably he knew that Mannering would not let him keep up the pressure any longer, and that he'd learned as much as he could from his attempt at surprise.

'That's about right,' he said grimly. 'And I don't want you to run into trouble. I didn't know the girl was here: I came to see you.' His eyes were calculating, enough to set Mannering's pulse beating faster. 'I don't know what particular job you're doing for Theodorus Wray. I don't know whether he's persuaded you to protect him and the girl while he's in England, but he's made a lot of enemies, that much I do know. And as far as I can judge, he's a ruthless operator on world markets. He's also so pleased with Mr High and Mighty Wray that he seems to think that he can get away with anything. Well, he's wrong.' Bristow was very gruff. 'I don't want you to get yourself entangled any further with him. I think we'll be able to prove that he killed Odell, but if you quote me, I'll deny having said it. I'm telling you for your own good.'

He sounded as if he meant it.

'Thanks, Bill,' Mannering said. 'But you could be wrong. If you got to know him, you'd rather like the chap.'

'He wouldn't be the first killer I liked,' Bristow said, with grim humour. 'Let me tell you something that will shake your belief in the mastermind. We know he had a local telephone call about ten minutes before he left the hotel. We know that he made an appointment with Odell at a place specified as "her place". We've got this from two sources: first from Odell's wife, who was with her husband when he made the call from his apartment: second, from a hotel operator who listened in to part of the conversation. The operator was holding a call from Japan on the line, and wanted to see if she could interrupt the conversation. She says that the tone of the men's voices was such that she didn't feel that she could. Wray rang off, but called her a moment later to postpone the call from Tokyo. Even you couldn't be such a lunatic as to ignore that kind of evidence. And even if you gave it to Wray's lawyers, it wouldn't help them. But don't let a word get into the Press, or you'll be held up for contempt of court.'

'So you've a warrant out for Theodorus Wray,' said Mannering heavily.

'Yes,' Bristow declared, 'and we're going to get him soon. If you do anything to shelter him, you'll be neck deep in trouble. I've a couple of men outside,' he added. 'Mind if they have a look round here? We're already searching Quinns.'

Chapter Sixteen

Spell?

Twenty minutes afterwards, the two Scotland Yard men whom Bristow had called in left the flat, after reporting that there was no sign of Theo Wray. Bristow looked at Mannering with a kind of grim amusement as the door closed. Mannering kept quite straight-faced. 'Not guilty, you see.'

'If he gets in touch with you, and he probably will, let us know at once,' ordered Bristow.

He looked up as the telephone bell rang. There was an extension in Mannering's study, the door of which was ajar, and Mannering went into the small room, with its oak panelling and its centuries'-old furniture: a room which might have been entitled to a corner of Quinns itself. Bristow sat on an oak settle which was not exactly what it appeared to be; it was an electrically controlled safe, too small for a man to hide in.

Mannering answered the telephone.

'Hold on,' he said, and handed the instrument towards Bristow. 'For you.'

'Thanks.' Bristow leaned forward. 'Hallo? ... Oh, yes, Smart ... Not there? ... Yes, all right, tell them you were sorry to trouble them, and warn them to tell us if he shows up.' He rang off.

'So I'm not sheltering a murder suspect anywhere,' said Mannering dryly.

'Not yet,' Bristow said, and moved out of the study to the drawing room.

While the search had been going on, Rosamund had put on a little rouge, powder, and lipstick, and had brushed her hair. There was a scared look in her eyes, but she was much more herself. Bristow, seeing her made up for the first time, looked at her almost in surprise. There was a softer note in his voice when he said, 'Miss Morrel, it's your duty to inform the police if Mr Wray makes any attempt to get in touch with you. Failure to do so would have serious consequences, possibly for the two of you. I hope you understand that.'

'Yes, I do.'

'To your knowledge, did Mr Wray know Odell before today?'

'No.'

'Very well,' said Bristow. 'The same applies to all of you,' he went on, and added abruptly, 'Where is the diamond ring which Wray bought yesterday? The Red Eye of Love.'

'In a safe,' Mannering answered promptly, and didn't add that, a few minutes before, Bristow had been sitting on it. 'You don't think that's involved, do you?'

'I'm not sure what's involved yet,' Bristow said. 'I am sure that Theodorus Wray can tell us a great deal that we don't know.' He nodded and turned to go.

Mannering saw him out, and went back into the drawing room at once. He half expected Rosamund to ply him with questions, or to talk hopelessly and helplessly about Theo. She did neither: all she said was, 'He must be mad if he thinks I'd give Theo away.'

The tone of her voice and the expression in her eyes told Mannering that she believed that Theo had killed Micky Odell.

Certainly the police believed it.

The hunt was up, and from this moment on, the search for the fabulous millionaire would be going at full pressure. The evening papers would carry it, television and radio would probably make reference to it, for he was too sensational a character to be ignored. The morning papers would blazon the news. It was hard to believe that Theodorus Wray could hide for long. He'd had no time to get to airfields or to sea-ports: the call for him must have been out within an hour of Odell's death.

One thing, which Bristow hadn't mentioned, puzzled Mannering a great deal.

Who had tipped off the police, and sent them to visit Rosamund's flat?

Certainly not Theo himself.

So someone else had known that Odell was dead.

It was an odd fact, but true, that Thomas called Tom had been back to the Kensington flat for some oddments that Rosamund had left behind, and must have been there only a little while before the murder.

He could question Tom, Mannering told himself.

Or he could wait until the police got round to that.

He did not really suspect Tom. There seemed not the slightest motive, except that absurd one that Odell had threatened Rosamund. Yet it was true that from the moment that he had set eyes on her, Tom had behaved as if there was no other woman in the world.

It was absurd, it was ludicrous, it was fantastic, it was childish even to remember the history of the Red Eye of Love, and to know that its legend gave it a kind of hypnotic power, drawing men towards whoever owned it, men who would give their lives for the woman on whose finger it lived.

Why had he, Mannering, been so taken by Theodorus Wray almost from the moment he had first seen him?

Why had he slipped so naturally, so easily, into the role of unofficial guardian of Rosamund Morrel? For he had: and Lorna had.

Oh, it was normal and natural: Rosamund was so pleasant to know, anyone would want to help her, and yet – she'd caused a positive upheaval here. A girl whom they'd never heard of two days ago was installed in the flat, and Lorna was as worried about her as if she had been her own sister.

Or daughter.

There was a kind of fatal attraction towards her: a desire on Mannering's part to make sure that she wasn't hurt. He had been inwardly angry with Bristow because of the way he had questioned her.

Another odd thing: Bristow's voice had softened when he had last spoken to her, as if he had also come under her spell.

Her spell?

Spell?

There was much to do at Quinns, but it could wait. Mannering went there to talk to Larraby, and find out if Larraby had anything to report.

He had one thing, and it was damning: the story that Odell and Theo had arranged to meet was known by many of Odell's friends and associates, for his wife had told several, and the story had spread. Even the newspapers had the story, but it was doubtful whether they would use it.

'What shall we do if Mr Wray does get in touch with us?' Larraby asked, in the quietness of Quinns office.

'Arrange a rendezvous,' Mannering said promptly, 'and let me know at once.'

Larraby smiled.

Mannering found himself puzzled by his own reaction. He hadn't come to the decision about a surreptitious meeting by logical thinking: the words had come out unconsciously, as if no other course was open to him.

'I'm going over to the Panorama Hotel now,' he went on, and looked at his watch. It was nearly six o'clock, and the rest of the staff had gone. 'I'll leave you to lock up, Josh.'

'Very good, sir.'

Mannering walked briskly along the strip of carpet leading to the front door. Two young girls were looking at a jewelled comb which now lay upon the velvet, a comb so encrusted with diamonds that he could understand why one of the girls said, 'It can't be real.' But it was real. It had belonged to the Spanish queens in the days of the greatness of Spain's empire, and there was no other like it. In a few minutes, Larraby would take it out of the window, under the eyes of the night watchman, who was a comparatively recent acquisition. The alarm systems and the burglar-proof devices at Quinns were so complex that Mannering seldom gave serious thought to the risk of burglary.

Mannering's car was parked near Hart Row. The streets were emptying by the time he reached it, and he was soon at the Panorama Hotel, overlooking Hyde Park, on a lovely May evening without a cloud in the sky. Half London seemed to have decided to take advantage of the change in weather. Every seat and every bench was occupied: thousands sat on the grass, which was vivid green from the winter's rain; thousands more strolled beneath the trees, which were just unfurling bright green leaves, as though they had given themselves a good shake and were waking for the summer.

Mannering was known at the Panorama, as he was everywhere in London.

He saw a Yard detective in the foyer, another near the lifts at the end of the sumptuous entrance hall, a third at the seventh floor, where Theo Wray had his suite, a fourth in the passage outside the suite. This large man, with a round-shaped head and startled blue eyes, knew Mannering and smiled as if this arrival didn't surprise him at all.

'Evening, sir!'

'Hallo. Mr Wray turned up yet?'

'I wouldn't be here if he had.'

'That man is full of surprises,' Mannering said. 'It wouldn't astonish me if he came back dragging the murderer by the collar.'

'Don't you think he—' The man was startled into a question that was both indiscreet and foolish, and checked himself in time.

'Of course Wray didn't kill Odell,' said Mannering, in so confident a voice that he knew that the plain-clothes man would not only tell his colleagues, but put it in the report for Bristow.

Mannering rang the bell, and almost at once a middle-aged, capable-looking woman opened the door: she had iron-grey hair, a beautifully ironed white blouse, without any frills, a neat black skirt. Inside the suite, Charley Southpaw Simpson was talking on the telephone in that quiet, courteous voice: but Mannering thought there was a note of exasperation creeping in.

'... I'm afraid I don't know when he'll be back.'

'Good evening, sir,' the grey-haired woman said, standing with a hand on the door as if determined not to allow him to pass. 'I'm afraid that Mr Wray is not in.'

'I'd like to see Mr Simpson. My name is Mannering.'

The shiny, rather rugged face cleared. 'Oh, Mr Mannering! Please come in. Mr Simpson has been hoping to get away to see you, but the telephone never seems to stop ringing, and—but you can imagine the difficulties, can't you?' She positively smothered him as she closed the door, and her voice dropped and her cheeks reddened a little more. 'I hope you won't think me impertinent if I tell you what a pleasure and an honour it is to meet you. It's like meeting a famous film star, or a general, or – if you know what I mean.'

Mannering's eyes were smiling with her.

'I do, and it's charming of you, but there's really no cause for it.'

'Oh, I don't agree with you! Some of the investigations you have conducted, often in defiance of the police – well, in my considered opinion, they make you an outstanding personality. I've assured Mr Simpson that if anyone can help to absolve Mr Wray from this crime, it is you. Of course, Mr Wray didn't do it. The very idea is absurd.' She led him through a sumptuous apartment to a great room with an enormous window overlooking the park: and, standing at a desk, with an expression now of annoyance more than exasperation, was Southpaw Simpson.

'I'm covered with confusion, really,' went on the secretary, 'because I didn't recognise you the moment I saw you. Unfortunately so many people have attempted to get in on one pretext or another that I was suspicious. Ah, Mr Simpson has nearly finished.'

'No, I don't,' growled Southpaw, and banged the receiver down. Mannering remembered that in the ring he had sometimes looked as he did now, with a frown that was not quite a scowl, and would soon break into a smile. It did. Simpson came forward, with a massive shrug of resignation. "Thank the Lord you've come to see me; I don't think I'll get away from this collar and chain all night. All right, Miss Bettley, go back on guard, will you?'

'I think I ought to remind you, sir, that Mr Wray was quite definite about the New Fortune shares. He wanted to sell them today, and we did not do so. However, Mr Courtney said that he was interested in private dealing. Shall I get him on the telephone?'

Simpson said, rather slowly, 'No, I don't think so. I can only push everything off until Mr Wray gets back.'

'I don't wish to make difficulties, but Mr Wray was quite definite about it. You will have to make some decisions sooner or later.'

'When they're necessary, I'll make them,' Simpson said sharply, and Miss Bettley tightened her lips and went out, closing the door. Charley Simpson stood near the window, looking over the park. Mannering felt the attraction of the lovely sunlit scene, stretching far into the distance yet in the midst of London.

He was quite sure that Southpaw Simpson wasn't thinking of the scene.

'The devil of it is that she's right,' he said. 'I've got to make decisions sooner or later, and later means tomorrow. Theo had about thirty big deals pending. If I don't say yes by tomorrow, in most cases it will mean no. And if Theo comes back and finds I've lost him two or three million pounds—'

He threw up his hands in a hopeless gesture of resignation. 'Oh, it's crazy! Do you know, Mannering, I meant that? It's nothing I've dreamed up. The difference between the right and the wrong decisions on the matters pending will be close on three million pounds. I know that if you say it quickly it doesn't sound so much, but it's a hell of a responsibility.'

'Didn't Theo leave any guide as to what he was going to do?' asked Mannering. 'Notes, or records, or—'

'That's the trouble; it's almost impossible to interpret Theo to the average man who thinks in terms of notes and card indexes,' Charley said. 'The only card index he ever kept was in his mind. He's quite fantastic, and—' He broke off, and stared out over the green heart of London. His face was set and his jaws worked before he went on. 'It's hell to think he might spend the rest of his life in jail.'

Chapter Seventeen

Find Theo

'So you think he killed Odell?' Mannering asked quietly. Something about the thrust of Charley's jaw suggested that he wanted to refute that: but he didn't. He turned to look into Mannering's eyes, but it was several seconds before he spoke. Then it was slowly, and deep in his throat.

'I didn't say that, Mannering. I hope to God he didn't. I can't bring myself to believe that he would, although lately he's got into such shocking rages, sometimes he hasn't seemed to be himself. The very devil has got into him. He used not to be like that. He used to be indifferent to everything and everybody who opposed him. That was before he started thinking he was infallible.' Charley's voice quickened; he was almost challenging. 'I've been with him for seven years now. I was boxing in Melbourne, and we were staying at the same hotel. He'd seen me knock out a goodish man, and came straight up to my room next morning and offered me a job as his chucker-out. That's what he called it. He offered me five thousand pounds a year, free of tax. It was making money talk. When I realised that he meant it, I took the job. He doubled the salary after two years. Don't think me just a heel if I say that it's going to make a hell of a difference to me if he is put in jail.'

'That's a lot of money,' Mannering remarked.

'He's always talked big, since I've known him, and he's always behaved big. First he talked in tens of thousands, then it became hundreds of thousands, and three years ago he started to talk in millions of pounds. I can't say now how much he's worth, but it's a fabulous sum. He seems to smell anything which will make money. When he buys land, before you know where you are there's oil or uranium or diamonds in it. He actually bought a played-out diamond mine in British West Africa – the big boys had given it up – and he found a fortune within three months. It's crazy luck, and I've always been afraid that it wouldn't last. Don't get me wrong,' Charley went on, his voice sharpening again. 'It isn't all luck. Most of it is sheer courage – courage to buy big and sell on the rise. That, and his fantastic memory, and his way of picking hunches—'

'Charley,' Mannering interrupted, 'I'll grant you all this about Theo. When did he start throwing these fits of rage?'

'As I told you, soon after he began to think he was infallible. I think he's driven himself too far. He hardly sleeps, by normal standards. Three or four hours a night is his average, and I've seldom known him to sleep five hours. He's often worked right through the night. He seems to have some kind of dynamo inside him, which drives him on and on and on. It's crazy for a man with so much money to go on trying to make more, but that's what he does all the time.'

'Isn't it the only thing he can do?' Mannering asked.

Charley looked startled for a moment, and said in a wondering voice, 'I hadn't seen it that way before. You mean, he can't do any of the ordinary things, like golf, swimming, tennis – goddammit, he doesn't even drink or smoke!' Charley's eyes became strangely bright. 'He's dedicated himself to making money, in other words, and got so deep into the habit so that he can't get out of it. When he's not thinking in digits, he's restless, can't concentrate on anything else, except—'

'Rosamund.'

Charley gave his expansive grin. 'That's right! She's heaven-sent. I've never known anything to take Theo's mind off the stock market and real estate until he saw her. It was frightening, really. I was at this cocktail party when they met. It was just another party, thrown by an old friend of Theo's and Rosamund came late. Theo saw her come in. It was as if the moment he set eyes on her he said: "I want her; she's mine." He's said that about a lot of things before, but never about women. Before the evening was out, I knew what he was going to be like, and I was as nervous as a kitten in case she didn't see it the same way, or was married.' Charley shrugged. 'All right, in case she was lying in wait for him. Everywhere that Theo goes, the gold-diggers are sure to flock. When I saw how things were going, I could hardly believe the luck. It looked as if he was ready to take a rest, and do nothing but go about with Rosamund. I could have kissed her for it. He even began to look better, wasn't so tight-lipped, lost the lines round his eyes. Then he got the crazy idea of doing all the work he'd planned for the next three months in three weeks, so that he could have a long honeymoon.'

'Do you think he's just overtired? Or is he afraid of being attacked?' Mannering asked.

'Sometimes I think one way, sometimes another.'

'Has he told you he's afraid of being attacked?'

'Sometimes. People he's beaten on the market hate his guts.'

'Anything recently?'

'No.'

'When did he first start losing his self-control?'

'When we were using a little broker in New York,' Charley said. 'He never liked dealing with big firms; they would always argue, and he didn't want to waste time. He told this chap to buy some stock, and the man thought he'd said sell. The broker claimed that he said, "Get rid of it", not "Get it", but I don't think Theo would make a mistake. I'm sure he wouldn't blame any man for something he didn't do. That kind of integrity has become God to him.'

The picture of Theo Wray was becoming much more vivid even than it had been before.

'What happened to the New York broker?'

'Theo walked out on him, after accusing him of deliberately selling him short. That was just before he left for England.'

'No signs of nervous strain before then?'

'No,' answered Charley. 'It was about then he saw a doctor in New York, and got this tranquillising drug. It works, and he's better than he was. I tried to stop him taking the tablets, but you don't argue too much with ten thousand pounds a year, tax free. I did take one of those tablets to an analytical chemist. They're okay – not really habit-forming.'

'Has Theo been worse these past few days?'

'Ever since he started overworking again.'

'Are you sure it's the overwork, or is something else bothering him? What about the men who attacked him outside my flat – did he tell you about that?'

'Yes,' Charley said. 'And he told me they made cracks about Rosamund. I see what you're driving at,' Charley added thoughtfully. 'Was he being needled into killing Odell?'

'Or doing something violent that would get him put away for a while.'

'Revenge by one of his victims? Could be,' conceded Charley.

'Do you know who it might be?'

'No. I'll dig a bit.'

'Make it as soon as you can,' Mannering urged.

'I will,' Charley promised, and added almost awkwardly, 'He had one of his sudden enthusiasms about you and Mrs Mannering, you know. He decided that you were the absolute tops. I can see what he means. I only wish that I could do something to help him in this jam. Er—I have power of discretion up to a point,' Charley went on. 'I can sign cheques and make purchases up to certain limits, for instance. I hope you won't want to pitch me out of the window when I say that the sky's the limit for fees, if you'll try to help him. I can guarantee that. And I could advance up to five thou.'

'Forget it,' Mannering said. 'I couldn't drop this affair now if I was paid to.' That remark came without thinking, too; it was as if someone had put both thought and words into him. 'Have you any idea at all where he is?'

'No,' answered Charley flatly.

'I shan't tell the police, if you have.'

'Mannering, if I had an inkling, I'd tell you. I haven't the faintest idea. I had to give the police a list of all his business contacts, and could let you have a copy of that. I can't tell you anything else.'

'What about this old school friend who threw the party where he met Rosamund – Norman Kilham, isn't it?'

'Yes, there's Norm,' mused Charley. 'I only know that he was an old friend, and that Theo consulted him on tax problems. I expect the police have talked to Norm by now,' Charley went on. He thrust his hands deep in his pockets. 'I suppose you might be able to squeeze more out of Norm than the police, if he had a guilty conscience. Care to try?'

'I think I'd like to know where Norman Kilham lives, and learn more about him,' Mannering said. 'He seems the only line we can work on.'

'Yes,' agreed Charley, but he didn't seem too sure of himself. 'You might try Rosamund, of course; I'm sure Theo's told her more than he's ever told me. She might—'

He broke off when the telephone bell rang, and glanced at the door, obviously expecting Miss Bettley would answer it in the other room. Then both of them heard her exclaim, heard her come rushing towards the door and fling it open, crying in a loud voice, 'It's him – he's on the telephone. It's Mr Wray!'

Chapter Eighteen

Orders

The woman's voice echoed triumphantly about the great room, a ringing: 'There, I told you so!' Charley's head went back, as if someone had struck his chin, taking him completely by surprise; but that did not last long. He swung towards a telephone at the desk where he had been sitting.

Mannering was already on the move. He passed Miss Bettley, and saw a telephone with its receiver off on a table in the outer room. He picked it up and stood waiting for Charley and Theo to speak. The woman came hurrying in, saw what he was doing, and said, 'Oh!' in a vexed voice. Mannering covered the mouthpiece and said to her, 'I might be able to find a way to help if I listen in,' and immediately she seemed mollified.

All that took only a moment.

'Hello, boss,' Charley said in a casual voice. 'I wondered when we'd be hearing from you.'

'Well, stop wondering and get your pencil,' Theo said, his voice no whit changed in vitality and firmness. 'The dogs are after me; I can't stay in this box long. Ready?'

'Yes.'

'Nagtyko: sell at fifty-five shillings today, don't load the market, sell at fifty shillings tomorrow, and then get the best you can for them. Supra Texas Real Estate; buy all you can at a limit of two dollars an acre, you ought to get it for much less, use Cyrus in

Houston to handle it for us, keep away from that goop in New York. Buy South African gold. Buy Australian gold and uranium. Sell Australian wool; prices are going to tumble, they've had a record growing year and that means a record clip. Check a little firm in Walsall, England, name of Gregory, Fish & Son—got that?—and find out if you can buy a controlling interest quick. They've got a genius up there who's got a new petrol-saving carburettor which is real good, and some ideas which will make millions. Name of Jones. Don't let 'em know it's Jones you're after, don't over-offer at first; they're not fools, but they are in financial trouble. Sell Chicco coffee and buy Tip-Tap tea, without limit, only don't spoil the market.' There was a moment's pause and what sounded like a rustle of paper, and then Theo went on in exactly the same strain, orders pouring out of him like water from a tap. Or water from a mountain spring, it was so natural.

Then Theo switched from one subject to another with only the slightest of pauses.

'That's that. Get Bettley to work late today and tomorrow again, pay her double, and promise her a bonus ... How's Rosamund?'

'She's all right.'

'She at Mannering's place?'

'Yes. Theo—'

'It isn't that I don't want to listen. I just haven't time,' Theo said. 'Any minute now the cops will plant their heavy hand on my shoulder if I don't get out of this box ... Ask Mannering to keep Rosamund at the flat. Don't let her go anywhere. If she has to leave, have two men following her. Anyone who will do this to me will do anything – including killing Rosamund.' Now his voice was icy cold, and it was possible to imagine the way his nostrils were nipped, to imagine the pallor about his lips. 'Tell Mannering it doesn't matter what it costs, provided he—'

'I've told him already.'

'Thanks, Charley,' Theo said, and paused for a moment as if he wanted the other man to know that he was really grateful. 'And tell Mannering I'm going to telephone him at his flat tonight, as near nine o'clock as I can make it. Just after dark – I can get out more safely then. That's all. I'll be seeing you.'

'Theo,' Mannering interrupted, 'why did you kill Odell?'

Theo actually drew in another sharp breath, as if not only surprised but badly shaken. When he answered, there was an angry note in his voice. 'You must be crazy. I didn't kill Odell.'

'You're about the only one who thinks you didn't, except Rosamund,' Mannering said. The rider seemed to be tacked on by someone else; he hadn't meant to say it.

'God bless Rosamund. And goddam you if you think—'

'Were you at her flat this afternoon?'

'Listen, if I don't go—'

'If you go I'll wash my hands of the whole business and the police will put you in jail for the next fifteen years,' Mannering said roughly. 'Get this into your head: you're wanted for a murder which it looks as if you committed. If I'm to help, I've got to know the facts.'

There was hardly a pause before Theo said, 'Fact one: I didn't kill Odell. Fact two: I did go to Rosamund's flat. Fact three: Odell invited me, saying (a) he wanted to show me something that might make me change my tune about Rosamund, and (b) sell me information about a plot to ruin me. Fact four: if he'd been alive when I arrived, I might have killed him. Fact five: someone got in first. Fact six: if you're going to try to prove to the police that I didn't kill Odell, go and see a man named Cunningham, Jack Cunningham. He lives in Park Court, near Grosvenor Square. Shake the truth out of him. Fact seven: I didn't know it, but I ruined Cunningham two years ago, and as a result his wife committed suicide. Fact eight: Cunningham has a daughter, Diana, who married Micky Odell a few months ago; she was the blonde last night. Fact nine: if you can find time to fix this on Cunningham, fine, but give priority to Rosamund.'

'About this Cunningham,' Mannering said abruptly. 'What else can you tell me about him?'

'I'll call you around nine,' Theo promised.

'Theo!' Charley shouted, as if he knew that was the only way to prevent Theo from ringing off. 'You can't leave it just like that. The police—'

'I'm going to talk to the police right now,' said Theo, and rang off. Charley gasped.

There was another sound, as of the rustling of paper; then a sharp click followed Theo's abrupt departure. Mannering had no doubt the police had been listening in, that there was a detective at the switchboard of the hotel.

If Theo did ring Scotland Yard ...

It was exactly the kind of thing that he might do. Here was a man who knew that he was wanted for murder, knew that the police of the nation were on the lookout for him, yet he could telephone those orders to Charley, his mind crystal-clear, and could cheerfully contemplate telephoning the police.

Mannering found himself smiling, and saw Miss Bettley's pop-eyed curiosity; in a moment she would burst out with questions.

Before Mannering had replaced his receiver Charley was striding in, his eyes blazing, his fists clenched. It was easy to believe that he had taken Theo's guilt for granted, but that now he believed him innocent, and believed that he might be saved.

'Did you get that about the man named Cunningham?'

'I got it,' said Mannering, 'and we won't broadcast this – but we'll take Miss Bettley into our confidence.' So he placated Miss Bettley, who gave a little giggle of a laugh. 'I'll see what I can find out right away.'

'Fine,' said Charley, and gripped Mannering's forearm. 'I can easily understand why Theo took to you; you're the first man he's ever met who works as fast as he does. Right! I'd better get busy.'

'Come down to the lift with me, will you?' Mannering asked, and urged Charley with him, into the passage. Then, quietly: 'All I wanted to say was that you mustn't tell Miss Bettley any details about Cunningham. Just stick to the business.'

'You're just as bad as Theo,' Charley said with a sigh. 'He always labours the obvious too. What's the betting that she'll tell the first newspaperman she comes across that Theo called?'

Mannering did not go straight out of the hotel, but to the telephone exchange, which was tucked away on the ground floor behind several public telephone boxes. The plush luxury of the hotel did not extend to the switchboard, where some tattered telephone directories were on a counter which was scratched and in need of a repolish. Two girls were at the huge switchboard itself; a dozen calls were in; one girl was saying, 'Please hold on, New York, our caller is waiting.'

In one of the telephone boxes, Mannering saw a Scotland Yard officer whom he knew slightly; and this man was almost certainly reporting to the Yard.

A girl, nicely made-up, nice-looking, earphones on and mouthpiece like a small phonograph fastened to her chest and moving wherever her head moved, looked up at Mannering. 'Can I help you, sir?'

'Yes,' Mannering said, and his eyes smiled; he knew that the girl would be easy to impress. 'Did you take Mr Wray's call just now?'

She looked startled. 'Mr Theodorus Wray?' She meant to stall, and looked at the box where the detective was talking.

'Yes,' said Mannering, and handed her his card, hoping that she would be even more impressed: if she recognised the name, there was an even chance. 'Did you take it?'

'Yes, sir, I did—oh, Mr Mannering.'

'Mr Wray bought his fiancée's ring from me, as you probably read in the newspapers,' said Mannering, and went on in the same easy voice, 'Was the call from a prepayment box?'

She hesitated.

'Was it?' Mannering insisted.

'Well—well, Mr Wray said that it was,' the girl declared, and coloured furiously. 'I had instructions to listen in, sir. But now I come to think of it, I didn't hear the coins drop in the box, and of course you always do with a prepayment call. I was taken so much by surprise that I hardly gave it any thought.' Her eyes glinted decisively. 'No, it wasn't a prepayment call.'

'Thanks very much,' said Mannering.

She would tell the police, but that didn't matter. The police would almost certainly assume the obvious: that Theo had wanted to fool them, Charley, and anyone else who might be listening in. Theo wanted them to think that he had left his hiding place in order to get to a telephone, whereas in fact there was a phone where he was hiding. It would be like him to confuse the trail just as much as he could, like him to pit his wits against the police, taking it for granted that he must let no one know where he was, in case the police made them give him away. He would stay free every possible second.

But he was somewhere with a telephone handy.

It was impossible to trace calls through the automatic exchange, so that wouldn't help the police.

It might help Mannering, because one thing was certain: Theo would go nowhere by chance. Wherever he went and whatever he did would be carefully calculated, like every risk he took. He would have some idea of the thoroughness and intensity of the police search, so – where would he hide? In the most unlikely place, of course, some place where he could be almost sure that the police could not suspect.

Where?

It would not be at the home of this man Cunningham, because Theo would be sure that the police had overheard that conversation. It wouldn't be at Norman Kilham's; that was too obvious. The police would almost certainly be on their way to Cunningham now and it would be a waste of time for Mannering to go there unless he wanted to let the police realise that he was working for Theo Wray.

That would mean a clash with Bristow.

Was Bristow at the Yard, or on his way to Cunningham's Park Court flat?

The news that Micky Odell had married the daughter of a man whom Theo had ruined was an odd twist, but didn't seem to affect the immediate problem:

Where was Theo hiding?

About ten minutes earlier, in Bristow's office overlooking the Thames the telephone had rung. He had put a cigarette down carefully on an ashtray, glanced at the inspector who was on duty in the office with him, and said, 'I wonder who this is?' and then announcing himself: 'Bristow.'

The inspector was stifling a yawn.

The yawn faded into astonishment, for Bristow looked as if he had received an electric shock. He sat bolt upright, and for a moment didn't speak; then he said shrilly, 'Put him through.' He waved at the inspector, who knew that he was being told to pick up the other telephone, and he did so. 'It's Wray, asking for whoever's in charge of his case,' mouthed Bristow. 'Hallo, this is Superintendent Bristow.'

'Hallo, Superintendent,' greeted Theodorus Wray in a bright and friendly voice. 'I don't think we've met; just as soon as we can I mean to put that right. It's a privilege to have a top man like you looking for me.'

'Mr Wray,' said Bristow, as earnestly as he could, 'I want you to understand that, if you come and see me, everything you say will be most carefully considered.'

'Everyone's innocent until he's found guilty, remember,' said Theo. 'Thank you, sir. I'll come and see you the moment I know for certain that you've caught the murderer. Right now I'm informing you that I am not the man you're after. All the time you look for me, you'll be wasting your time. That's simple fact. And will you—'

Bristow's voice grew almost shrill. 'Mr Wray, please listen to me!'

'You just get on with your job and I'll get on with mine,' said Theo brightly. 'I don't want you wasting taxpayers' money, and I'm sure you don't want to. But there's one thing you can do for me, Superintendent.'

'Mr Wray, everything you will say will be taken into account—'

'That's fine, we'll talk about it later,' promised Theo. 'Just now, I'm only anxious about my fiancée. I wouldn't like anything to go wrong with her, and if someone hates me so much that they'll try to frame me the way they have, Rosamund might be in danger. I've asked John Mannering to look after her, and I'm also asking you. If anything happens to Rosamund Morrel,' Theo went on, in a sharper voice, 'I shall hold you personally responsible.'

He rang off.

Chapter Nineteen

The Hiding Place?

Mannering went first to the apartment where Norman Kilham lived. Kilham was there, with his unexpectedly plump and placid wife. There seemed nothing remarkable about Theo Wray's school-days' friend, who seemed to be both shocked and grieved by Odell's death.

'I was in Brighton for lunch, didn't leave until four-thirty,' he said. 'I first read about it in the evening papers.'

If he had told the police that, it would stand up.

Mannering asked if he knew Cunningham, and Kilham answered promptly, 'Oh, yes, I handle the old boy's accounts – in fact I introduced Micky Odell to Di Cunningham. She'll be properly knocked over after this. I tried to see her, but she was with the police.'

There might be more to learn from Norman Kilham, but Mannering knew it would take a lot of digging out, and this wasn't the time for it. He left, and soon pulled up outside Park Court, which was not far away from the Panorama Hotel. He found a parking place for his Allard, just then the car of his choice. He was not surprised to see Bristow's car outside, nor surprised to see a plain-clothes detective standing with the commissionaire. It was over an hour since Theo had finished talking to him and Charley, and already dusk was creeping over London, although the sky was clear of cloud.

The Yard man nodded recognition.

'Mr Bristow still with Mr Cunningham?'

'He's still in the building, sir.'

'Thanks,' said Mannering, and went into the large hall, almost as plush, as the Panorama Hotel, with a thick pile carpet, a hushed atmosphere, panelled walls, gilt mirrors, silent lifts, and wide passages with alcoves all along them, a lovers' seat in each alcove: purely for show, of course. As he approached the main lifts, each with its diminutive uniformed attendant, one opened, and Bristow stepped out with two of his aides.

There was a hint of a smile in his eyes, although his voice was hard. 'I thought I told you to keep off this job.'

'I can't,' Mannering said simply. 'I doubt if I could if I wanted to. It mesmerises me.'

'That's the tallest story I've ever heard from you,' Bristow said, yet he didn't look as unbelieving as he sounded. 'Well, it won't do any harm to tell you that you're wasting your time here.'

'Cunningham confessed?'

'Cunningham flew to the United States yesterday afternoon, and is said to be going on to South America,' Bristow declared. 'He expects to be away from six to seven months. His secretary says she has no reason at all to believe that he'll be back earlier. He's a widower, with no ties. She also tells me,' went on Bristow, very quietly, 'that Cunningham lost a fortune in an oil deal about two years ago, and his wife, who was ailing then, died soon afterwards. Cunningham always blamed the losses for her death – and blamed the man who caused those losses.'

Mannering said, 'Theo Wray.'

'Yes.'

'So Wray knew what he was talking about.'

'It could be even that Wray's right, and that Cunningham is behind all that's happened,' Bristow went on, 'but a man who flew to New York yesterday – I've checked that he left London, no doubt about it at all – certainly didn't kill Odell this afternoon.'

Mannering said mildly, 'If you go on at this rate, the police will be doing quite a job before they've finished.'

'I don't think this is the time to be facetious,' Bristow said, and barked, 'Do you know where Wray is?'

'Didn't your man tell you exactly what passed between us on the telephone?'

'If the years have taught me anything, they've taught me not to take anything about you for granted,' growled Bristow. 'Do you think Miss Morrel has any idea where he is?'

'I don't think anyone has, Bill. I think Wray would make quite sure that no one could guess.'

Bristow nodded. 'Something in that,' he conceded.

Mannering said, 'Well, thanks for saving my time here,' and they walked out to the street together.

Mannering went to his car and drove off ahead of the police – and would not have been surprised had he been followed. He was not. That suggested that Bristow did not seriously think that he knew where Theo was.

He kept coming back to what seemed the only guide: that it would be the last place that he or the police or anyone else would expect. Somewhere with a telephone. Not a hotel or a boarding-house, because the police could cover all such places quickly. Therefore, a private house, or flat: private premises of some kind. There was nothing to suggest that Theo had prepared a hiding place while he had been in England; he hadn't had time, and as far as Mannering knew, there had been no need for it.

He drove to Green Street.

Two plain-clothes men were in the street, and he knew that another was at the back of the building, on the bombed site which was used as a car park. Bristow was doing two things: making sure that if Wray tried to get into Mannering's apartment, he would be stopped; and making sure that no harm came to Rosamund.

There was no sign of Thomas.

Mannering went up in the lift, let himself in, and immediately heard Thomas's voice, and, a moment later, Lorna's.

'… if you're sure, Mrs Mannering.'

'I'm quite sure, Tom. Miss Morrel won't leave the flat tonight without Mr Mannering's knowing. You've seen the police outside, and you know that we couldn't be more strongly protected.' There was a note of amusement in Lorna's voice that Mannering rejoiced to hear. 'You go home, and don't worry. Go to Quinns first in the morning, unless we get in touch with you.'

'Well, if—' Tom turned round, and saw Mannering. His eyes lit up. 'Oh, hallo, sir! I was just saying that I ought to go and see my people at home. We've some relations here from the north.'

'You carry on,' Mannering said.

"Thank you, sir. But if I thought there was the slightest reason to feel that I'd be taking risks with Miss Morrel, I'd make my excuses at home like a shot.' He looked at Rosamund as he spoke, and in his eyes was the light of adoration.

Moth to a candle?

Had she some deep, unsuspected, perhaps unwitting quality which did attract men, so that all they wanted was to make sure that nothing could harm her?

Nonsense!

'I know you would,' Mannering said to Tom, 'but there's no need to worry. You get along, and we'll see how things are in the morning. We won't leave Miss Morrel unprotected.'

'That's fine,' Thomas said with forced heartiness. 'Goodnight, Mrs Mannering. Goodnight, sir. Goodnight—er—'

'Goodnight, Tom,' Rosamund said.

Tom's eyes were glowing as he left the flat.

Mannering closed the door after him and went into the drawing room, where Lorna and Rosamund had already gone. Lorna looked her normal self: Rosamund looked a little pale, perhaps a little scared, too: certainly there was no happiness in her; no one could doubt that she was desperately worried about Theo.

Could they?

'John,' Lorna said, 'I think if Rosamund had her way, she would take the Red Eye of Love and throw it in the river!'

Mannering pretended to look shocked.

Rosamund tried to laugh. 'Nothing's gone right since Theo had the idea of buying it. It's almost as if it's cast a spell.' She gave a little shiver, which seemed genuine, and went on, 'I know it's ridiculous, and it can't be the ring. I just can't see anything clearly, I'm so scared. John, will you answer a question truthfully?'

'Yes.'

'Do you think Theo killed Micky?'

Mannering said., 'No.'

Her eyes didn't light up, as he had expected. She stared at him reflectively, as if her mind was quite clear, after all. 'I think you're saying that just to reassure me. I'd much rather know what you think.'

'I think that he went to the flat to see Odell, and found Odell there dead,' Mannering said. 'I know that Odell telephoned him, and persuaded him to go to the flat. Some person we don't yet know knew he was going there, and got there ahead of Theo. It could have been someone who wanted Theo blamed; it might have been someone who wanted to kill Odell.'

At last the brightness was back in Rosamund's eyes, and she exclaimed, 'You really do believe it!'

'Yes, I believe it,' Mannering assured her, and told them what had happened.

Before he had finished, Rosamund was saying in a dazed way, 'So he is all right. He's not hurt.'

'Wherever he is, he's as bright and lively as ever,' declared Mannering, and looked at her very straightly. 'Have you any idea at all where he might be?'

'If I could even guess, I'd tell you.'

Mannering believed that she would.

It was after dinner, which they started about nine o'clock, and while he was still pondering over the one question which mattered, when a ring came at the front-door bell. Mannering went to answer it. He wasn't surprised to see Charley Simpson. Charley had changed into a dark suit, and looked almost as if he were going to a church service or a funeral, but there was a glint in his eyes and an air of confidence which had been missing when Mannering had seen him at the Panorama Hotel.

'Hallo, Mrs Mannering. Hallo, Rosamund.' He gave her a brisk wave. 'I've laid on everything that I can, and arranged for radio-telephone calls to be put through here if any more come, but there should be a lull between now and eight in the morning. Then I can get cracking on the boss's orders.' He rubbed his chin as he went on, 'I even had time to read up everything I could about the Red Eye!' He glanced at Rosamund's empty engagement finger, and went on ruefully, 'He'd hate it if he knew it wasn't there.'

'He'd have more sense,' Rosamund said.

'Amazing story behind it,' Charley went on, and added with a little twist to his lips, 'The real trouble seems to have started since he bought the thing. It's almost as if it does cast a spell of some kind. Er—do you think it would be possible for me to have a look at it? The thing seems to have an hypnotic effect on me, even though I've never seen it.'

'It does on everyone,' Rosamund said gravely.

'Is it handy?' asked Charley.

'I can get it,' Mannering said, and when Rosamund nodded, he got up and went out.

He was in the study, about to open the electrically controlled oak settle-cum-safe, when Lorna came hurrying.

'Hallo, sweet,' he said. 'You want to get under its spell too?'

'Are you sure you should take it out?' Lorna asked. 'Isn't it better locked away?'

Mannering looked at her, and then very deliberately winked. She was puzzled, until he winked again. Then she laughed, and her face cleared. 'Oh, I see,' she said, and went out of the room.

'So that's it,' said Charley, looking at the ring as it lay in the velvet case, as if sleeping. 'All this fuss for that.' He peered more closely. 'I suppose I shouldn't say so, but it doesn't strike me as being so wonderful. I suppose I expect the fire to step out and burn me up, that's the way Theo talked about it. He said that it seemed to come alive when you put it on, Rosamund.'

Rosamund said very firmly, 'Well, I'm not going to put that on my finger again until I know that Theo's safe and free. I'm not sure that I will then.'

'Probably wise,' conceded Charley, and tapped his fingers against his mouth. 'Well, I'd better get back for some shut-eye; if I'm not up and about by seven in the morning I'll never catch up with the day. There's still a lot to do, and old Bettley's battling on. Amazing woman, that – got a remarkable mind for figures. Great stroke of luck that Theo managed to get hold of her. But then, he always does have the luck.' He stood up.

Mannering saw him to the door, and as Charley stood on the threshold, he looked beyond Mannering to the partly open door of the drawing room, and said in a quiet but urgent voice, 'I really came round to make sure that Rosamund's all right. Don't take the slightest risk with her, will you? Since this trouble blew up, I feel as if nothing matters but keeping her safe.'

And this had 'blown up' since Theo had bought the Red Eye of Love.

'We'll look after her,' Mannering assured him, and watched him go, then turned back into the study, lifted the telephone, and dialled a Chelsea number: the private number of Superintendent William Bristow. He was not surprised when Bristow answered in person, sharply: he would probably take it for granted that an eleven-o'clock call was from the Yard.

'Bill,' Mannering said, 'Theo Wray seems to have been very lucky with his temporary secretary, one Miss Bettley. She was absolutely right for the job, almost as if she was hand-picked. It might be worth checking where she came from and all about her.'

'Not a bad idea,' Bristow said at once. 'I know she came through an agency and her credentials seemed all right, but I'll probe. What's the matter, can't you sleep?'

'I keep waking up and wondering where Wray is.'

'If we find that you're giving him shelter, or know where he is, you're going to be in the dog-house,' Bristow said, and added very softly, 'I've been through all the reports taken since the murder. I've discovered that three people saw a man answering to your description in that street this afternoon. One of my sergeants remarked on the fact that it was probably you. Don't get yourself in the dock for Theodorus Wray, John. Don't persuade yourself that you couldn't be wrong about him. If a man with a mind like his has taken a wrong turning, then he'll use anyone and anybody to help him get his own way. There isn't much doubt he has a touch of megalomania: he can't bear being thought wrong.'

That wasn't Charley's view, but Mannering didn't argue.

'Be more specific, Bill. Whom do you think he'd use?'

'I said anyone and meant it,' Bristow asserted. 'Simpson, for instance, is now having to carry out Wray's specific instructions, and is doing so blindly. Apparently he always has. You seem to be eating out of his hand. Wray would use Simpson, he would use you, I believe he would even use Rosamund Morrel, to get what he wanted.

'Make sure he doesn't fool you, John.'

Chapter Twenty

The Last Place He'd Be

Lorna was in bed. Rosamund was in bed.

It was after midnight, and Mannering was sitting in his study, staring at the locked settle-safe, seeing Theo Wray's face in his mind's eye, grappling with the problem which had now become an obsession. Where was Theo? Bristow could say what he liked, but it was hard to believe that Theo was the Machiavellian mind behind all this: there could be no point in it if he were; but no one could be sure he knew what went on in Theo's mind.

Where was the last place he'd expect to be found?

Here? No, that was nonsense, although the police were half prepared for him. Rosamund's place? He would know that the police would be watching, and they had been in possession all day, anyhow. This was absurd: he was too tired to think clearly or he wouldn't have such nonsensical ideas. But it would be somewhere like that. Perhaps he had planned it beforehand, so that he had a secret hiding place to go to. He'd been warned of trouble by these chance encounters.

Mannering stood up, yawned, and went to switch out the light. He actually touched the switch when he caught sight of the headline of an evening paper.

MAY FAIR SOCIALITE MURDERED

Odell could never have wanted a better obituary. A number of Mayfair people wouldn't exactly be pleased, but they were unimportant.

Odell had made progress because he had amassed a fortune – not a fortune in the same sense as Theo Wray, but one which enabled him to rent the most expensive apartment in London.

There was the last place anyone would expect to find Theo. In Odell's flat!

Mannering forgot that he was tired, and felt as if he had been given a shot in the arm. He stood quite still, looking at the headline, then turned the newspaper over. There was a photograph of the block of flats, only ten minutes' walk away from the Panorama Hotel, where the lowest-priced apartment cost over four figures a year, and where some cost treble that sum.

Odell's flat?

It was there, in the heart of Mayfair. It was modern. It had a night staff of porters and two night-duty detectives, there to be on constant guard. It housed some of the wealthiest people in London, and many from abroad. The value of the costly furs and jewellery in that block of flats was probably greater than in any other single place in the whole of England, perhaps in the whole of Europe. And because of that, the owners had boasted before it had been built, and boasted now, that it was burglar-proof.

Was that where Theo was hiding?

The police would have been to see Odell's wife, of course, and had undoubtedly taken the chance to search the apartment, but once that had been done, they were likely to have only a formal interest in it. Odell's wife would have the best possible legal advice, and so the police would have to tread with great care too.

Was that where he would find Theo?

Mannering left the flat by the Green Street entrance, and knew that his departure would be reported to the Yard, but he wasn't followed. A call to have him watched might be put out, and radio cars and police on beat duty could trace everywhere he went – for just so long as he wanted to be traced. He drove the Allard to Victoria, parked it, and checked that he wasn't followed. He walked in the darkness of a side street, then swiftly towards a district of little houses, a few small factories, and some garages, which were closed for the night. There were lock-up garages among them. He waited near a lock-up garage, and no one came, no policeman's footsteps sounded, there was nothing to indicate that anyone knew that he was here.

A strange thing happened, a metamorphosis which came slowly, almost catching him unaware; and with it there was excitement and a sense of exhilaration, as if he were on a high peak, surveying the great mountains all about him, and setting out to climb the inaccessible, to do the impossible. He was not fully aware of it, but such moods as this, coupling danger with daring, made Mannering what he was, made him different, made him the man Theo Wray had liked because they had so much in common.

If the job had to be done, nothing must stop him.

And he drew upon the knowledge he had acquired in the deadly days that had passed.

There was no sound as Mannering pushed back the sliding door of the lock-up garage where he kept an old Austin with a specially tuned engine, capable of remarkable speed. This was one insurance against such difficulties as he faced tonight. He stepped inside, and paused to listen, putting care highest among the virtues. A car passed and people walked along a nearby road, but none came here. He closed the doors, and, knowing they were lightproof, switched on a light. He checked the tyres, the battery, and the oil, switched on the ignition, and confirmed that the petrol tank was half full. Once every two or three weeks he came here, to check all this.

It was cold.

He switched on an electric fire, and then set to work. Stored on a shelf was a theatrical make-up outfit. Inside a small hanging cupboard, a suit of clothes which was too large for him now; but there was an inflatable belt, which made him look fatter, and pads for his shoulders, so that when he put this coat on he would look older and round-shouldered. He stripped down to his vest, opened the make-up case, and set to work. It was a year since he had made up, but he had once been so familiar with its intricacies that it was like second nature. He could almost hear the voice of the old make-up expert who had taught him.

'… the important thing, Mr Mannering, is to use your natural features as part of the new appearance … make every feature a little larger, nothing even a little smaller … When you are going out among the people in the streets, be sparing especially with make-up at the eyes. There it is always more easily noticeable. Just narrow the eyes, and so change their appearance. Use a little of this quick setting gum in the corners … no, no, no, it will not make you look like a Chinese! And remember, the part of disguise which cannot be seen is always the best. Pads inside the cheeks, a film of this newfangled plastic to work over the teeth and gums, so … Little round pads for the nostrils …'

How long ago had this been, for him to have called plastic 'newfangled'?

Mannering was absorbed in what he was doing, and felt deep satisfaction when he saw himself change in front of his own eyes. He was plump, elderly, tired-looking, his eyes narrowed as if he were perpetually squinting and should wear glasses.

He changed his clothes, stripping right down: vest, pants, trousers, shirt, collar and tie, shoes, socks – everything; and he changed the accessories too. He could never be sure that he would not be stopped, held, and searched, and never be sure that the time gained by concealing his identity when he was first detained would not prove invaluable.

'… the little things, Mr Mannering, will make all the difference between a long life, or a short life not so merry!'

Suddenly a car engine sounded, turning off the distant Vauxhall Bridge Road. Mannering stopped working and listened, and his heart began to thump. The car drew nearer, and was slowing down. There was surely no reason in the world why the police should come here now. The car was crawling in low gear.

Mannering kept absolutely still, his teeth clenched so tightly that his jaws hurt.

The car went past, and was some distance off when its engine stopped. It was going to another lock-up garage, of course.

He began to pack his ordinary clothes into a large suitcase, taken from the boot of the car, and made sure that everything was in it, and if the police came here they could never tell that Mannering had occupied the garage. He put the filled suitcase in the back of the car. Then he drew on a pair of tight nylon gloves which fitted like another skin, but did not leave any fingerprints. He switched off the fight and opened the sliding doors, which were oiled so that they made very little sound.

Big Ben boomed.

One ...

The note quivered into the quiet of the night.

He had been here less than an hour when he drove the car out, closed the doors, drove to Victoria Station, and left the suitcase of clothes and oddments at the all-night parcels and left-luggage office. Then he bustled back to his car. His rounded shoulders and thick waist made him unrecognisable. A few of the station staff glanced at him – so did two policemen just outside – but no one took especial notice. He drove without haste through a London that was almost deserted. The Panorama Hotel was an oasis of light in abysmal darkness, for the great park carried no lights. He parked near the block of flats where Odell had lived, making sure that he had a position from which he could drive off in a hurry.

He took a tool-kit from a compartment in the car, with every tool he was likely to need tonight in its own place, each item checked and tested when he had last been at the garage.

Everything was ready.

Now he had to break into the building which was said to be impregnable, had to get into Odell's apartment, and find out if he was right.

Chapter Twenty-One

The Burglary

A few people were about, an occasional taxi passed, and a few cars. Mannering walked briskly, like a man on lawful business, towards Park Court. He could see inside the spacious entrance to the uniformed commissionaire. In the doorway of a Georgian house opposite, a man was standing with almost suspicious stillness. That would be a Yard officer, so the flats were under observation.

Mannering had expected that.

Yet his heart began to thump.

He walked past, and took the first turning on the left. The great building looked pale, with its light grey stone, against the night. Here and there lights were on, but most of the windows were in darkness. In the dark windows lay Mannering's greatest hope. Man could invent every kind of burglar alarm, but had not yet overcome the greatest single security risk: the house owner or occupier. Windows would probably be unlocked even if they were not left open. And here on a chilly May night, half of London's eight millions would have a window open several inches.

The building took up the whole of one block. There was another entrance on the parallel street, and a man would be watching there too. On this side was a high wall, with trees beyond it, leaves rustling faintly. Here were street lights. Behind Mannering a taxi trundled, and when it passed, he saw a couple clinging to each other on the back seat. Silence followed. He came to the tradesmen's entrance of the flats, and the main gates were closed, but a small gate set in them was open. He stood listening, and heard footsteps on the other side of the door. A man drew nearer. Mannering stood very close to the wall, so that he could not easily be seen if the man came and looked outside.

He did not, but passed the door.

Mannering moved inside swiftly. The man was walking with slow, deliberate steps away from him, clear in the pale light from the apartment building. Mannering went straight across to the nearest patch of black shadow. The police were taking extreme care, as if they too thought Theo might be here. More likely, they were watching for any of Odell's associates who might come.

There was a drive on to a steep ramp running down to the garage and the tradesmen's entrance. Would that be watched inside as well as outside? The patrolling figure was still in sight, walking away. Mannering slipped out of the protecting shadow, to the ramp and down it. He kept close to the wall. The ramp was so steep that it was hard to go slowly and cautiously; once, he almost pitched forward. There was no sound below, but there would be at least one all-night garage hand, and much more likely two. Cars would be coming in and out at all hours.

He heard a car engine being revved, saw the glow of headlights near the entrance to the ramp. He jumped the last two yards, and swung round the corner. Two cars were parked close to him, and he darted behind them, catching sight of a stocky man in overalls who was standing over a car which had the bonnet up. The arriving car came down the ramp at crazy speed, jolted to a standstill, and made the garage hand turn round and glare. A middle-aged man opened the door of the car, and said in a mellow voice, 'Here we are, m'dear, soon be tucked up in beddy!' He hiccoughed. The garage hand came over without enthusiasm. 'Put my car away,' the tipsy man ordered, and helped his wife out; she was younger, dumpy, and plump-breasted.

'Yes, sir,' the garage hand said.

The couple moved off towards the lifts, and the garage man got into the car and began to drive to the far end of the huge garage, using only the sidelights. Mannering kept moving between cars so that he could not be seen. The lift doors opened, then swallowed up the couple. He reached the lifts: there were six in all. The car was still moving, and the hum of the engine filled the low-ceilinged cellar. Mannering pressed the button of the nearest lift, and another button lit up, announcing: 'Lift Coming.' It was still coming when the car engine stopped, and he saw the brake light go on. In a moment, the garage hand might get out.

The lift came, and the doors opened automatically.

Mannering stepped in, and pressed the button for the fifth floor, for the telephone directory gave the Odell number as 516. He drew his hand across his forehead as the lift rose. It came away wet with sweat. There was a chance that the lift would stop at one of the other floors; he couldn't be sure. A bell clanged softly past each floor – three, four, five. It stopped. He stepped out, half expecting to see a man at the landing.

No one was in sight.

Notices on the wall showed not only where the different flats were situated but also showed names. He soon found:

Odell, M ... Apartment 516.

That was to the left. He went along, without hurrying, prepared to meet a member of the night staff or a Yard man, but he didn't think the Yard would be so careful inside the building as they were outside: they were checking all who went in and out. He reached the corner of a wide passage, with the thick pile carpet and the panelled walls, the cut-glass chandeliers – all the opulence one could expect – and no one was there.

Ten minutes after entering the building, he was at the door of Odell's apartment.

He bent down and examined the lock, for locks had many telltale signs. This was not only a double lock, but of the most modern type, the kind fitted when the latest invisible-ray system was used to detect burglary. It would be impossible to get inside while the door was locked, and it would be a waste of time trying.

At the end of the passage was a window, with rich red velvet curtains drawn. Mannering put out the passage lamp, and the only light left was a glow from the corner. He drew back the curtains to uncover the window, and examined it: there was the wiring system with a control switch, so each window had individual control.

He switched this one off and opened the window.

There was the darkness of the park in the distance and, nearer, street lamps, the headlamps of a car coming along towards the main entrance, and the glow of the lights at the entrance: so this flat faced the street, and a man was in a doorway opposite, watching. He might glance up here.

Mannering opened the window wider, and began to smile. There was no balcony, the drop to the ground was sheer, and if one fell, the chances of escaping alive were almost non-existent. But close by was a balcony outside a room of Odell's flat. It was four feet away, and so within a tall man's reach.

It did not occur to Mannering not to try to reach it.

He pressed close to the window, and drew the curtains behind him, so that there was no risk of being seen from the passage. Then he climbed out, clinging tightly to the window frame. He did not look below: he had to take the risk of being seen from the street. He judged the distance to the balcony, edged as far as he could to one side, then let himself fall sideways, with his arms outstretched. He had to fall to the left. Now that the danger was most acute, he was free from both fear and emotion. If he missed his grip he would fall; but it did not occur to him that he would miss.

His hand touched the metal of the balcony, and his fingers closed about it. The rest would be easy. He leaned all his weight on the iron rail, and twisted round until he was able to get his right arm round, and grip with his right hand. Then he hauled himself to the balcony with a single movement, and swung himself over.

He was safe.

Now that he was here, crouching against the wall, his heart began to pound and his breath to come in short gasps. The sweat on his forehead and on the back of his neck felt cold in the night's wind.

He stared at the houses opposite, expecting the quiet to be broken by a shout or the shrill blast of a whistle, but no sound came.

He hadn't been seen.

He looked at the window which led to the balcony. If the current had been switched on inside this window, then the best hope was to cut a pane of glass and grope inside until he found the switch: and he might need to cut not one but several panes. He glanced up. There was a fanlight, open a few inches and all fear went; all tension faded.

If a fanlight was left open, the current probably wasn't on.

It wasn't.

Mannering forced the secondary lock of the French windows in less than three minutes, stepped inside the apartment, and closed the doors behind him.

He stood absolutely still, listening for the slightest sound; if anyone was sleeping in this room he would be able to hear the breathing. He heard none. He switched on a pencil torch, and its narrow beam spread about the room: a small room, with books on one wall, a television set reflecting the bright orb of the torch, the beam, and Mannering's shadow. There were armchairs, and there was the smell of Turkish tobacco.

Mannering checked the position of the door, and crossed to it.

He opened it, and light came from the entrance hall, soft and yet, after the darkness, almost dazzling. He kept the door open an inch. He thought he heard voices, but could not be sure. He went into the hall, seeing four other doors and a small passage; and one of the doors led to the main passage outside. He stepped swiftly to this, saw the control switch, and pressed it down. Now he could open the door quickly, and if he had to run for safety, could get out at a moment's notice.

He stood listening, and there was no doubt of a man's voice. The sound seemed to come from a door next to the room from which he had come, another room with a front aspect. He stepped towards it. Yes, a man spoke, and then a woman said, 'No!'

It was impossible to be sure whether it was a cry of alarm or the cry of someone who was a little tipsy. Mannering stood still, trying to hear what the man said next. All he could catch was a faint rumble of sound. It stopped again, but this time the woman didn't speak.

Mannering turned the handle, very slowly.

If the man or the woman were looking this way, he or she would probably notice it.

Theo said, in a tone at once gentle and hard, 'You don't know me, honey, or you wouldn't say a thing like that. You've got me all wrong.'

'I know your kind,' the woman answered, and undoubtedly she sounded frightened. 'You're all talk, and you won't do anything about it.'

'Now, honey, isn't that unkind,' Theo jeered.

Now Mannering had the door open wide enough to see inside. The blonde widow was sitting on a couch, with one leg drawn up beneath her, wearing a dark dress which threw the smoothness of her arms and legs and shoulders into bold relief. She was the blonde who had been at the Signet Club with Micky Odell. She was sideways to the door, and Mannering recognised her on the instant.

Theo was standing and looking down at her. He was smiling. In his right hand he held a small, dagger-like knife, hidden from the girl behind his back.

Once, Mannering had felt sure that Theo Wray would never use a knife.

Now he moved so that the girl could see it, and that was when Mannering saw fear leap into her eyes.

Chapter Twenty-Two

Blonde Widow

Mannering could thrust the door wide open and make Theo swing round, could distract his attention with a shout, a call, even a quiet word. He did none of these things. He opened the door a little wider, but not enough to step through. The blonde was staring up into Theo's face, and the fear in her eyes seemed to touch lips which were drawn back over her teeth. Yet she looked more striking than she had at the Signet Club: fear gave a character to her face. She didn't move, and Mannering saw the way in which Theo moved the knife gently forward, the point towards her breast.

'Don't get me wrong, Mrs Odell,' he said. 'I mean business.'

She tried to press back against the silken cushions; and the cushions and the couch were all that Mannering noticed of the lovely room, one meant for millionaires.

'I know you mean business,' she said chokily. 'But when you killed Micky, you killed yourself. I don't care what you do to me; I wouldn't say a word to help you.'

'You might regret that,' Theo said.

She couldn't get another inch away from him, and he was creeping closer. She tried to stare him out, but could not. Mannering could only see Theo's profile, that lean, graceful body, and the blade of the knife which was so much nearer the pale flesh.

'I wouldn't regret it as much as you would,' she said. There was a funny kind of catch in her voice, almost as if she were trying to laugh in spite of her fears. 'You're finished, Wray. You're through. Micky said he'd finish you.'

'Not yet,' Theo said. 'Not by a long way.'

Mannering pushed the door wider, and squeezed through.

The girl was more likely than Theo to see him, but she did not see him yet; she could only look into Theo's face, and then glance fearfully towards the knife.

'Micky set out to ruin you, and we'll finish the job,' the blonde said. 'Nothing you can do can stop it!'

'I can stop it,' declared Theo. He stopped; and the knife kept still.

Mannering could see his profile – in fact, could see more: there was a beading of sweat at Theo's forehead and upper lip, and he was very pale. He moistened his lips with the tip of his tongue. Theo in a wild fury might kill, but Theo wasn't the calculating kind of killer, and had no appetite for this. As he watched, Mannering began to realise that Odell's widow suspected that, and felt less afraid with every passing second. The fear faded from her eyes, and her lips slackened; she stopped pressing back against the pillows.

'You won't kill me,' she said flatly.

'I'll kill you,' declared Theo, but it was clear that he would not, unless something happened to spark off the rage which could burn him up. 'You've just time to tell me who killed Odell, that's all. Because if I'm to be blamed for Odell's murder, I might just as well add yours to it. That way I'd get punishment for something that I did do. Don't underestimate the danger, Diana dear.'

She actually leaned forward, and her voice was full and venomous. 'You'll never find out who killed Micky! You'll never find out a thing.'

'Wrong,' Theo asserted. 'I've been finding some things out while I've been searching this fine apartment. I know that you're Abe Cunningham's daughter, but Cunningham didn't kill Micky Odell; he was already out of the country. I know that when your father heard that I was corning to England, way back in December, he began to plan to fix me, baby. He started with Norman Kilham, but Kilham couldn't help, except to send him on to Micky.'

There was a pause, before Theo went on. 'That looked as if it would pay off, didn't it? And you and Micky got married, to celebrate in advance. It was to be a squeeze that would dry me right out, and when I fell for Rosamund you had all the answers – or thought you had.

'Too bad Rosamund wouldn't play it your way, wasn't it?' Theo demanded harshly. 'Too bad my nerves didn't crack, in spite of the tough guys Micky sent to work on me. Too bad I had a shadow named Charley Simpson, who taught me what I needed to know about judo and boxing.'

Theo caught his breath, and when he continued, his voice was pitched on a higher plane. 'And too bad I didn't fall for your talk about killing your mother too. Want to know something, Mrs Odell? That bothered me for a while; I discovered that I had a conscience. But since I've been here I found out your mother died of cancer which she had had for years before I ruined Abe, so my conscience got right up again.'

'Your conscience,' Diana Odell sneered. 'It won't keep you out of prison. And look where you are now. You daren't show up tomorrow, because the police would get you at once. You've got to stay in hiding. While you're in hiding, you'll lose everything you've got.' She actually laughed, and there was a kind of courage in her: it was as if she was defying Theo to strike. 'In just a few days you'll be ruined, because you daren't show your face to the world. It's a nice way of getting one's own back, Theo dear. You ruined my father, you killed my mother, and now you've killed Micky. I don't care if you kill me. I don't care if I don't draw another breath. All I want is to make sure that nothing can save you.'

'If you knew who'd killed Micky, it might help.'

'I won't help you, and no one else can.'

Was that deadly, murderous fury building up in Theo now?

Mannering could see the way his lips were set, and his nostrils began to narrow and go white. But it might not be with fury; it might be with fear. Odell's widow meant exactly what she said, and no one could gainsay her courage.

There was only one good thing.

She knew who had killed Micky Odell, and it hadn't been Theo Wray.

Had Theo been going to strike, he would have struck by now. He didn't. He probably felt vicious with the girl because he was standing there like a fool, while she mocked him. She was smiling into his face, and there was a glint of triumph in her eyes.

That was the moment when Mannering let them know he was present.

He did not speak in his normal voice, but used a grating one which made him sound a much older man. 'For a price,' he said, 'I might help you, Wray.'

The girl turned her head with a startled movement, and actually started to get up. Theo spun round, the knife glinting, but there was no threat in the movement, only absolute astonishment.

He looked into the face of a stranger.

'Who—' he began, and broke off. Mannering had never seen him utterly flabbergasted before; at another time that might have been a memorable sight.

Then Odell's widow moved.

She thrust Theo backwards off his balance, sending him staggering. She bounded off the couch and rushed towards Mannering and the door. She swerved suddenly to try to get past him. He grabbed at her, touched her arm, felt the soft, warm flesh, then lost his grip. She reached the door, which was still open. If she reached the front door and the passage, even if she managed to lift a telephone and cry for help, she would bring the police swarming here. Mannering pivoted round and ran after her. She slipped through this door, and tried to slam it in his face, but she could not. She darted towards the front door, which he had left unlocked and easy to open for his own escape.

She was just out of reach.

She touched the handle of the front door.

Mannering reached her, clutched her shoulder and pulled her back. She kicked and struck and clawed at him, but could not get away. She gave one scream, but before she could repeat it, Mannering had her fast with one arm, and smothered her cries with his free hand. Then Theo came. Mannering lifted the girl off her feet, and Theo clapped his hand over her mouth. They took her into the room from which they had come, and Theo closed the door. Mannering put the girl on the couch, and then drew back, his right cheek smarting from a scratch, and breathing hard.

'Vixen is the word,' Theo said tautly. 'What's the word for you?'

'Friend.'

'The kind of friend who would cut my throat.'

'The kind of friend who thinks you'll pay well for help.'

'Maybe you're right,' said Theo, less harshly, 'but the help would have to be good.'

'Try me,' Mannering suggested.

Theo did not press his questions, but was very wary as he looked at the girl again.

'What's your price for help without any argument?'

'You won't be able to pay anybody's price,' said Odell's widow in a gasping voice.

'You forget that you need a few days to complete his ruin,' Mannering said, in that harsh, unfamiliar voice, 'and you won't have them when we find out who killed your husband.'

'You'll never find out.'

'You didn't think that Wray would kill you,' Mannering said very softly, 'but you can't be sure about me. There isn't a thing I wouldn't do for money, and Wray can pay me all I want.'

She was frightened by that, and Mannering did not think that she would be able to throw this fear off so quickly: but she would try. It had looked as if Odell had married a clinging vine, but she was a fighter, and it was impossible not to admire her.

'You've said I can pay,' Theo said tautly. 'Just name your price.'

'He'll never be able to pay you,' Diana Odell said harshly. 'Tomorrow he'll be in jail and there'll be panic selling of his shares – not only here, but all over the world. Once that starts, the bottom will fall out of the markets he's in, and he'll be in trouble, he'll be so deep in trouble that he'll never be able to get out. Even if he's let out of jail and tries to save the bottom from falling out of his market, he'll have to sell his real estate. But once the slide's started there'll be no stopping it. I know exactly how it works.' She was almost breathless. 'I had to stand by and see it work with my own father. He was one of the richest men in the country until Theodorus Wray started to work on him. Wray played the markets until my father was compelled to sell all his land, all his property, everything he possessed to try to stop the rot. But he couldn't. And do you know why? Because he'd bought too much of some big stocks, and when he started to sell, the price just went down to zero. Wray forced it down. Wray thinks he controls an empire, but it'll soon start crumbling away. He himself might be able to hold it, but he won't be there to try. Why, I've already had word that the news that the police are after him had started a wave of selling in Australia and New Zealand!'

She stopped; and the silence in the room seemed heavy and ominous.

Wray looked at the girl without speaking, and Mannering felt that it was almost superfluous to ask, 'How right is she, Wray?'

'I couldn't be more right,' the girl said, and fear had gone in this new kind of bitter triumph. 'He hasn't a chance unless he's on the spot to handle the situation for himself. He's the great one, he's Midas the Memory Man, he's the one who keeps everything in his head, he's the one who makes millions by balancing one million against another.'

'Anyone who knows what holdings I've got and what property and real estate I own could do it,' Theo said in a strangely quiet voice. 'Sure, I did this kind of thing to Cunningham, but he was trying to fight me. I offered to buy him out. He wouldn't sell, so it was war. That's just a different way of fighting. It went my way. If it had gone his way, I would have been in trouble.'

'You couldn't be in worse trouble than you are,' Odell's widow said viciously. 'You haven't a chance to save yourself from losing all you've got – your money and your liberty, perhaps your life. What does it feel like to be on the receiving end, Theo?' How she sneered.

Theo said in that unexpectedly quiet voice, 'I don't like it much, but I've been there before.' He looked up into Mannering's face, not knowing that it was Mannering, not showing the slightest sign of recognition. 'Someone told me recently that I had to face facts. The facts are that unless I can handle this situation myself, it can go the way she says. So I have to find out who killed Odell.' The beginning of a smile curved his lips. 'Or you have to, I don't seem to have the knack! Will you try?'

Mannering said: 'Don't you have an assistant? Can't he help?'

'Charley?' said Theo, and his lips curved still more and he shook his head. 'No, that's where my method hits back at me. Charley hasn't got the initiative or the courage for a job like this. He's got all the physical courage in the world, but when he starts juggling with big money he gets scared of the risk. It paralyses him. That's how I wanted it. I wanted a man who would do what I told him and never make any attempt to show me how clever he was himself. I talked to him earlier tonight. It was obvious he was standing by and waiting for me to tell him exactly what to do. But I can't handle this on a telephone, now.' Theo gave a choky kind of laugh.

'You can't handle this at all,' Odell's widow sneered. 'You haven't a chance in a million.'

'You might try by asking her one question,' Mannering suggested. 'Ask her if her father ever had a secretary whose name was Bettley, a middle-aged, grey-haired woman who talks too much and is always ready to show how bright she is by acting on her own initiative.'

Theo gasped: 'Betty!'

The girl lost her colour, but didn't speak.

'Betty,' repeated Theo, thinly. 'She's the brightest secretary I ever had. She's been with me just two months, and I'm quite sure how good she is. She knows all the answers. She knows world markets inside out. I was so lucky to get her I couldn't believe it. If it wasn't for her love of making decisions off her own bat, I'd have paid her a fortune to join me and Charley. Betty,' he repeated, and it was almost a groan. 'She knows as much about my holdings as anyone in the world except Charley and me.' He turned very slowly towards the girl on the couch, and asked in the same level voice, 'How about it? Did she ever work for your father?'

Diana Odell did not say a word, but for the first time since Mannering had seen her, her spirit seemed to fade.

'Wray, I'm going to talk to the woman, Bettley,' said Mannering abruptly. 'You keep trying to make Mrs Odell name the murderer.'

'Sure, I'll try,' Theo promised. 'Maybe it won't be so difficult now.' He looked straight into Mannering's eyes, which were gummed a little at the corners so that their shape was altered, and the pupils were enlarged because of drops, and looked quite different from Mannering's eyes. 'How come you're so anxious to help me?'

Mannering said, 'I've always wanted to be a millionaire.'

He turned and went out, knowing that both the girl and Theo were staring after him in the one thing they shared: bewilderment about him. He opened the door of the passage, stepped out, and closed it again without a sound. He turned towards the lift, but had taken only a step when he heard men walking, two or three heavy men, treading heavily enough for the thud of their footsteps to sound in spite of the thick carpet and the sound-absorbing walls.

He moved round swiftly, looking over his shoulder. He could still hear but could not yet see the men. He pushed the velvet curtains aside and stepped behind them, with his back to the open window.

Then the men appeared, three of them, and he recognised a Chief Inspector of the CID.

They headed for Odel's apartment, as if they knew exactly what they wanted and what they were going to do.

Chapter Twenty-Three

Who Killed Odell?

The three men stopped outside Odell's door, and Mannering, peering through a tiny gap between the curtains, saw one put his finger on the doorbell. Another man looked his way, then glanced up at the chandelier, which was in darkness. Mannering kept quite still, but a breeze was coming in at the open window, and he could not stop the curtain from billowing. If that detective noticed it he would come at once. Could he climb down?

The men still stood there, looking at the door, and one of them said, 'Try again, before we use the passkey.'

'I can't understand what makes you think that a search warrant was necessary. Surely poor Mrs Odell has suffered enough today.' So the speaker was from the apartments, not a Yard man.

A man said, 'We just want to make sure that Mrs Odell isn't hiding someone we want to talk to.'

The wind seemed a little fresher, and the man glanced at the curtain again. Did he notice anything? Mannering felt his heart pounding: the thudding seemed enough to suffocate him.

Then the door opened, and Odell's widow said, 'Who on earth are you?'

'I'm a police officer, Mrs Odell, from New Scotland Yard. I'm sorry to worry you so late, but we've instructions to come and search your apartment. Please don't make difficulties.'

He was fluttering a paper, doubtless the search warrant.

Mannering couldn't see the girl.

He did see the way the three men tensed themselves.

Then suddenly Theo appeared, corning like a bullet and looking as if he meant to force himself bodily through the trio. He sent one man staggering, brought the other to his knees, actually turned into the passage, and began to run. Then one of the men stretched out a leg and brought him down.

As he crashed, Mannering saw Odell's widow. She would tell the police about the visitor, and they would want to know why they hadn't seen him. They might come and look here.

One of them had snapped handcuffs on to Theo Wray, who stood very still, his face set; yet in some remarkable way he hardly looked dishevelled. At last he looked every one of his years. He was staring at the girl, who backed into the flat, saying, 'He forced his way in here! I couldn't keep him out!'

'You two take Wray downstairs,' said the man who had done most of the speaking. 'I'll have a word with Mrs Odell. Send Parsons and Jameson up at the double, will you?'

'Sure.'

Wray was marched off, at once.

The man went into the flat, but left the door ajar.

Mannering waited until he and his captors had vanished round the corner, then crept out of his hiding place, past the open door, and towards the stairs. He reached the staircase safely, and prayed that he would meet no one on the way.

He did not.

He went out boldly, and no one stopped him.

Theo was held between the two men who had arrested him, just outside the flats, and made to get into a police car. Mannering waited until it had driven off, and then walked briskly to his own car. In fifteen minutes, he was back at the garage, but never had fifteen minutes seemed so long, never had he lived so much in so short a time. He was not really normal until he was beginning to remove the disguise, and even then his mood was very subdued.

In half an hour, he was John Mannering again, and the most dangerous part of the great gamble had succeeded.

But the case wasn't over yet by a long way.

He left the garage at a little after four o'clock, while the night was still black and most of London still asleep.

He went to a telephone kiosk near the station, and put in a call to the Chelsea flat. There was no answer at first, which hardly surprised him. The bell went on ringing. There was none in the bedroom, but one just outside. Usually Lorna woke quickly; she must be sleeping heavily tonight. *Brr-brr-brr-brr.* On and on it went, and he began to frown, puzzled. Could he be ringing a wrong number? Perhaps he was tired, and had dialled quickly, without concentrating. He got his sixpence back, inserted it again, and dialled – with exactly the same result. This time there was no question of a wrong number. He felt his grip tightening on the telephone as the ringing sound went on and on. Someone would wake up and hear it, surely: and he could not remember a time when Lorna had not answered, if she had been able to.

If she had been able to.

Brr-brr. Brr-brr.

He put the receiver down and stepped outside. Suddenly he was frightened. A mist of rain was in the air, and he felt it cold upon his face, matching the sudden coldness in him. He went hurrying towards the station taxi rank, almost at the double. Police and porters watched, and a cabby leaned out of his seat to open the door.

'Green Street,' Mannering said.

It was a ten minutes' journey. Mannering sat back in the cab, hands clenched tightly, and lips set, looking into the misty drizzle, the haloes round the street lamps, the haloes round the lights of cars and the trucks and cycles coming towards him.

Soon they turned into Green Street.

'Wait, please,' he said.

No one was about. He could not be sure, but he did not think the Yard men were here now, and as Theo was in custody, their main purpose in watching the premises was gone. Mannering unlocked the street door. It was very quiet when he stepped inside the house, and only a dim light burned in the hall and on the landings. He stepped into the lift. Tension had never been greater in him than it was as the lift crawled upwards.

He stepped to the front door of his flat, inserted the key, hesitated, and opened the door cautiously. If there had been trouble here, someone might be lying in wait. He heard no sound, not even of breathing, and felt sure no one was in the hall. He pushed the door wide open, and stepped swiftly inside – and then saw a glimmer of light in the main bedroom, the door of which was ajar.

Lorna's name was on his lips, but he did not utter it. He crept across the hall to the door, listening for the slightest sound, but heard none until he reached the bedroom door; then it was the softest of soft breathing.

Lorna's?

He opened the door.

She was lying on the top of the bedclothes, in her pale green pyjamas. Mannering could see even at this distance that she was breathing. She did not seem to be hurt, looked as if she had got up, been searching for her slippers after putting on the tiny bedside light, and then dropped back to the bed, asleep. Why? How long had she been like this?

Her pulse was steady.

He left her, and turned towards the spare room, the door of which was wide open. He stepped inside, and switched on the light, and stared at the empty bed.

Claudia was in a drugged sleep too; but she did not look as if she had been disturbed.

Mannering lifted Lorna, put her down again, pulled the bedclothes over her, and then went out and down in the lift to the waiting taxi.

'Seen anyone about?' he asked.

'No. Expect someone?'

'I just hoped,' said Mannering.

The police had been withdrawn, and someone had come to the flat, picked the lock, drugged Lorna and the maid, and taken Rosamund off.

Mannering did not want to think about the alternative.

It was just possible that Rosamund had got up and drugged the others and left of her own free will. It was remotely possible that Rosamund had been involved in the plot against Theo, and that something had alarmed her, and she had decided to get away from the flat, perhaps from London, perhaps from the country itself.

And there was another possibility which he hated to think about.

No Scotland Yard detective was outside the Panorama Hotel when Mannering paid his cabby off. He went inside. The hotel was brightly lit; there were several commissionaires; there were page boys inside, lift boys, pale-faced men in black at the reception and the cashiers' desks. A little woman with a child asleep on her lap sat unexpectedly against a pillar, with several Pan American bags about her feet.

A boy took Mannering up in the lift.

A chambermaid sat dozing at a junction of passages. A waiter wheeled a trolley containing tea and toast along past her. Both wished Mannering good morning. He reached the door of Theo's apartment, and glanced right and left, making sure that neither waiter nor chambermaid had followed or were watching him. He saw no one. This was just a hotel-room door and simple to force. He made little sound, and pushed the door open only an inch.

He heard nothing.

The outer room was empty.

He stepped across, knowing that Theo's bedroom was on the right, Charley's on the left, and the main living-room-cum-office beyond, overlooking the park. The desk where Betty had been yesterday was tidied; a chair stood squarely behind it; and the telephone he had used was squared: whatever else, Betty kept her things in good order.

Mannering heard voices.

The door of the big room was closed. He put his ear to it, but couldn't distinguish anything except the fact that people were talking. He opened the door with the same caution as he had before, and looked inside.

A man and a woman were talking.

Charley Southpaw Simpson was talking to Cunningham's onetime secretary, Miss Bettley, Theo's find of the century. Mannering peered closer into the room. They were sitting together on a couch, and a trolley was in front of them, containing early breakfast.

Miss Bettley stretched forward to pour out tea when Mannering said, 'Good morning, folk. Where's Rosamund?'

He had never seen two people move more quickly or in such alarm. Charley was on his feet in a bound, and banged the table. A cup tippled over, and tea spilled from it, splashing on to the woman's lap, but she did not appear to notice, just gaped, open-mouthed.

Simpson barked, 'What the hell are you doing here?' and then raised his right hand as if he wished he were near enough to drive his fist into Mannering's face.

'I've told you, surely,' Mannering murmured. 'I'm looking for Rosamund.'

'She isn't here!'

'I don't believe you,' Mannering said. 'I want to know whether she came of her own free will, or whether you brought her by force or under duress. Where is she?'

'Mannering, you must be crazy.' Simpson lowered his arm slowly. 'We haven't the faintest idea where Rosamund is. Isn't she at your flat? I thought you were supposed to be looking after her. When Theo finds out—'

'Theo is in custody,' Mannering told him. 'When he comes out, he's going to find out a lot of things. For instance, that you killed Micky Odell. That you took Miss Bettley on as secretary, knowing who she was. That the pair of you planned Odell's murder between you, as you planned to ruin Theo. That with him in hiding or in custody you were going to flood the markets with stocks he owns and bring the prices crashing. Then you and Cunningham, probably Cunningham's daughter, and almost certainly Norman Kilham were going to buy at rock-bottom prices. The stocks are sound and are bound to recover. You were going to ruin Theo as he's ruined a lot of others – but he fought by the rules and you tore the rules to pieces.

'Why is it, Charley?

'Just for money? Just for love? Or do you simply hate Theo?'

Chapter Twenty-Four

Fair Rosamund

'You are crazy,' Charley said in a choky voice. 'Miss Bettley came in early because there's so much to do. We're going to carry out Theo's instructions. You heard what he told us to do; you were here when he telephoned.'

'It won't do, Charley,' Mannering said. 'You'll never get away with it. Will he, Miss Bettley?' He actually smiled at the woman. 'You followed Theo about wherever he went – when it suited you, Charley. When it didn't, you blamed him for avoiding you. Unlike Mary's little lamb, your skin's as tough as hide, and whenever Theo was in trouble, you didn't want to go. No one was ever surprised when you followed him, though; that was one of the things you were paid for. In some ways, you improved on the little lamb – on the occasion when you went ahead of Theo. You heard Odell make the appointment with him, went ahead, and killed Odell before Theo arrived.'

'I don't know what you're talking about,' Charley denied, and spread his hands. 'Theo gave me the slip.'

'You framed him, then came back here and pretended that you knew nothing about it,' Mannering insisted. 'It wasn't Betty; I knew she was in this suite all the time. It wasn't Rosamund, because she was at my flat. It wasn't Abe Cunningham, because he was flying to New York. It wasn't Diana Odell; she was with friends. So by a process of elimination we come to you.'

'It could have been any of a dozen people!'

'A dozen wouldn't know about Odell's visit to the flat and the rendezvous.'

'Odell's friends—'

'Who would want to kill him there and then?' asked Mannering. 'And who would believe that Theo would tell his friends that he was going to see Odell? Charley, I've been thinking about other things – especially why Theo went to meet Odell at the flat. He wouldn't go simply to hear accusations against Rosamund. He had the sense to know that if he got mad with Odell, he might kill him, and he didn't want to land himself in dock on a charge of murder. Odell was the very last man with whom he would make an appointment unless there was some strong overpowering reason why he should. There was some plot to ruin him, and Odell said he'd heard of it, and would sell his knowledge. Theo told me that.'

'You've seen him?'

'Never mind what I've seen, think of what I'm saying. Odell was going to sell Theo information about a plot: this plot. If Odell was in the plot, he wouldn't sell: so he was outside, but he knew about it. Who told him?'

'You're dreaming this up,' Charley growled.

'Odell's wife had reason to want to get her own back, and her father conveniently left the country,' Mannering went on. 'She's been heard to say she wouldn't name Odell's killer for any price. Know why, Charley? Because her husband found out what she was plotting. Whether he also found out that she didn't give a damn for him but was in love with you, I don't know. But I do know the basic facts. You and Diana Cunningham were in this, getting expert advice by remote control from Cunningham, and technical help from Miss Bettley. The essential condition for success was to get Theo out of the way. You tried, by needling him until he was living on his nerves. You employed men to attack him. You planned with Odell to find a girl who would help to crack him. Odell had his own game to play, of course; he didn't know he was a tool in your hands too.

'Theo thought that Odell had been murdered so as to frame him, of course,' Mannering went on in the same positive manner. 'And

Theo jumped the gun, not knowing Southpaw-Stab-in-the-Back was rejoicing. Charley, where is Rosamund? Did she come here of her own free will? And why did you hate Theo so?'

'He doesn't hate Wray; he just wanted to take as much money as he could,' Miss Bettley broke in thinly. 'He was the only one who didn't hate Wray. I did, because he ruined the kindest employer who ever lived. Diana did, because he ruined her father and killed her mother. Abe did too – but Charley didn't; he was just in it for what he could get. He killed Odell, to stop him talking and because he wanted Odel's wife. I know; I've seen him and that slut together. I didn't know he was going to kill anyone – I'll swear in God's name that I didn't know, nor did Abe. We just wanted Wray out of the way – we thought he'd go off with his Rosamund, and that would have been time enough, but when he decided to clear everything up before his honeymoon, something drastic had to be done.'

Southpaw Simpson leapt at her, and as she backed away, he turned on Mannering. He was as hard as a man could be; he had been a professional fighter for ten years of his life, and now came with hatred and with murder in his eyes, because it seemed that only Mannering stood between him and getting away.

Mannering took his hand out of his pocket and showed a knife.

'I shouldn't,' he said. 'Miss Bettley, telephone 999 and ask the police to come here at once.' He saw the woman, so used to taking orders, go to the telephone. He watched Charley, knowing that it would be only a moment before the man tried to get past him, defying the knife.

'Rosamund!' Charley cried. 'Rosamund, get him, get him quick!' As he spoke, he flung himself past Mannering, and had Mannering looked round, he could not have stopped the man. But Mannering didn't look round. He shot out his leg and tripped Charley up. He gripped the man's right wrist, forcing it behind him in a hammer lock. Then he let him go, spun him round, and cracked him under the jaw; and Charley's eyes rolled as he dropped, unconscious.

'I told you—' Mannering began to Miss Bettley.

'I'm going to,' she said gaspingly. 'I was afraid he was going to hurt you. He forced me to help him this morning, Mr Mannering;

he said if I didn't, he would kill me too. I just didn't know a thing about it ... Hallo! Hallo! ... This is Mr Wray's suite, will you please send the police here at once?' She put down the receiver noisily.

Mannering stood back from Charley and asked, 'Is Rosamund all right?'

'Yes, sir, she's unconscious, on Mr Wray's bed. He gave her a drug. I swear I couldn't help myself, Mr Mannering!' She was almost in tears. 'I hated Mr Wray at first for what he'd done, but I couldn't condone murder.'

'When you knew about the murder you could have turned Charley in,' Mannering said coldly.

'He frightened me into saying nothing! And—and my future depended on him. So did Mr Cunningham's. He had us where he wanted us, Mr Mannering. When he rang up and told me to come early, I couldn't help myself. And when I got here he told me he'd been to bring Miss Rosamund away, that if there was any trouble he would kill her too. I just couldn't help myself—'

Then there was a thump at the door. A moment later a house detective and two policemen came in ...

Rosamund lay in a drugged sleep, like Lorna and the maid at Green Street.

'I should say she'll be round by noon,' said the doctor who saw her. 'She'll be a bit tired after it, but she'll come to no harm.'

'Can she be moved?'

'Oh, yes, in an ambulance or in a car. She'll have to be carried down, though.'

Mannering went with Rosamund in the ambulance to Green Street, watched a nurse put her back into the spare bed, and waited while the doctor confirmed that Lorna and Claudia were suffering from the effects of the same drug, and there was no need to fear. Then he asked the Yard to send a man to guard the flat against emergency, and Bristow's night-duty opposite number promptly promised to send one round.

'Then I'd like you to come and see me, Mr Mannering.'

'Fair enough,' Mannering said.

He was at the Yard at half past eight, and Bristow was already there. Mannering told the police all he knew and had reasoned, and the police measured his statement against Miss Bettley's; that won an almost reluctant smile of approval – and a grin from Bristow.

When they were alone, Bristow said, 'What time did you leave Odell's apartment this morning, John?'

Mannering frowned. 'I didn't go near it, Bill. What's on your mind?'

Bristow was still smiling. 'Mrs Odell told a story of a man who broke in there and did quite a job of helping Theodorus Wray. She didn't place you, and her description doesn't fit you, but if you weren't there, I'm the Chief Constable.'

'Well, so you should be. I don't know who it was, Bill. Wray has a lot of odd friends, remember. Why don't you ask him?'

'He says he doesn't know who it was either,' said Bristow. 'Just says that he wants to find him so that he can give him a million pounds.'

Mannering whistled. 'I don't know who it could have been,' he insisted, 'but I wish I could make Theo Wray believe that it was me. Have you released him yet?'

'Released him! He was out of the Yard like a streak of lightning,' Bristow said. 'He waited only to make sure that Rosamund Morrel was safe, then went back to the Panorama. He says he wants to undo any harm that the others did, and he's probably got New York on one telephone, Tokyo on another, and Siam on one at his feet. By the way, Simpson has made a statement too. He knew it wouldn't be any use holding out in view of the Bettley woman's evidence. There's one thing you didn't know.'

'Just one?'

Bristow smoothed his brown-stained moustache and said, 'Only a trifle, John, but there has to be something! Simpson had one fear: that you might discover the truth. You knew more about the association between him and Wray than anyone else, and might realise that he was the obvious suspect. He wanted to make quite sure he could finish the job even if Wray was released. So he kidnapped Rosamund Morrel. He would have taken her out of the apartment if Wray had been released, and threatened to kill her if Wray tried to fight back. Simpson made an impression of a key from Lorna's handbag, went to your flat, drugged Lorna and the maid with a nasal spray with morphia in it, woke Rosamund, and told her that Theo was back at the hotel. She couldn't get there fast enough, and didn't dream that Simpson was in the plot against Wray.'

'Ah,' said Mannering. 'That was my chief worry: that she'd gone of her own free will. She'd got up and dressed; there was no sign of a struggle; and obviously she could have been in the plot.'

'I don't mind admitting that for once in my life I took a suspect's innocence for granted,' said Bristow. 'I don't understand it; I've never felt so certain about anyone before. If any of my chaps had told me that story, I'd have told him he was losing his grip. There's something about that girl—' He broke off, frowning, and asked sharply, 'What are you smiling about?'

'Guess.'

'I don't see why—' Bristow began, and then drew in a sharp breath. 'Damn you, no! That legend about the Red Eye of Love is an old wives' tale. There can't be anything to it.'

'If it isn't the ring, it's the girl, and if it isn't the girl, it's the ring,' Mannering said. 'Everyone wants to fly to Rosamund's side and become a little St George. You and me too. But it doesn't much matter, because we'll never be able to think of the girl and the ring apart.'

'Wray won't expect her to wear it all the time, will he?' Bristow asked, yet sounded as if he thought Wray was quite capable of that.

'Just in case of such an emergency, I had a replica made days ago, worth seventy-five instead of seventy-five thousand pounds,' Mannering said. 'I always like to have a dummy for show purposes. It's going to be my wedding present to Rosamund. She can tell Theo when she's wearing the real thing if she wants to. That everything, Bill?'

'Just one more warning,' said Bristow dryly. 'You'll soon be too old for acrobatics.'

'I gave that kind of thing up years ago,' Mannering declared, and went off from the Yard.

He went by taxi to the Panorama, and was eyed by everyone in sight until he reached Theo's suite. There a young man stood, as if on guard, but opened the door immediately he recognised Mannering.

Mannering went in.

Theodorus was in solitary state. He had a scrap pad and a stump of a pencil in front of him, and four telephones at hand. He was speaking into one, and to Mannering it seemed almost as if time had stood still.

'I'm not making any changes for three months,' Theo was saying. 'I'll sell if I think there's any need, but I'm not buying. I'm going on a honeymoon. Yes, sir, a honeymoon. Yes, right away; I'm not waiting for banns or anything else, I'm going to get married right away … Yes, I know I might lose a chance of making a fortune – I don't want to make any more fortunes for three months … Yes, thanks very much … Goodbye.' He rang off.

He beamed up at Mannering. 'Hi, John,' he said. 'That's the last business call I intend to make for three months or more. Know where it was from? You'll die laughing. My London lawyer's home, in Grosvenor Square! My, you look as if you could do with some sleep. Been up all night? I'll ring for some coffee, and then we can go to Green Street and see how Lorna and Rosamund are getting on. Don't misunderstand me, I've made inquiries; but asleep or awake, I like to gaze upon Rosamund's face – and the ring on her finger too.' He smiled, and moved to the great window, looked over the green beauty of Hyde Park, the few people in it at this hour of the day, the traffic in Park Lane, and the panorama of distant London. He put a hand on Mannering's arm, and was much quieter and more subdued than Mannering had known him. 'Wonderful city,' he declared. 'Wonderful place. Hasn't got the exhilaration of New York or Sydney, but it gets a hold on you. Like you do. Typical of your kind, John, aren't you? At least, half of you is. I'd like to get to know that other half better.'

'You're dreaming,' Mannering said. 'Which other half?'

'The half to which I owe a million,' Theodorus said, and his smile was the smile of a very wise man. 'The one with a scratch on his cheek.'

He looked at the scratch Diana Odell had made on Mannering's face.

And he winked.

John Creasey

Gideon's Day

Gideon's day is a busy one. He balances family commitments with solving a series of seemingly unrelated crimes from which a plot nonetheless evolves and a mystery is solved.

One of the most senior officers within Scotland Yard, George Gideon's crime solving abilities are in the finest traditions of London's world famous police headquarters. His analytical brain and sense of fairness is respected by colleagues and villains alike.

'The finest of all Scotland Yard series' – New York Times.

Gideon's Fire

Commander George Gideon of Scotland Yard has to deal successively with news of a mass murderer, a depraved maniac, and the deaths of a family in an arson attack on an old building south of the river. This leaves little time for the crisis developing at home ....

'Gideon of Scotland Yard emerges as one of the most real working detectives in modern fiction.... A sympathetic and believable professional policeman.' - New York Times

JOHN CREASEY

THE CREEPERS

"The prisoner's hand was thin and bony ... And in the centre of the palm was a pinkish mark. It was the shape of a wolf's head, mouth open, fangs showing. Although it was what he had expected to see, Inspector West felt a twinge of repugnance a stab not unrelated to fear. It was the fifth time he had seen the mark of the wolf – the mark of Lobo."

A gang of cat burglars led by Lobo cause mayhem as they terrorize the city. They must be stopped, but with little in the way of evidence the police are baffled. Just how can Inspector West manage to do this in what is a race against time before more victims succumb?

"Here is an excellent novel of law enforcement officers, harried, discouraged and desperately fatigued, moving inexorably ahead under the pressure of knowledge that they must succeed to save human lives." - Cleveland Plain-Dealer

"Furiously exciting" - Chicago Tribune

"The action is fast, continuous and exciting" - San Francisco News

JOHN CREASEY

THE HOUSE OF THE BEARS

Standing alone in the bleak Yorkshire Moors is Sir Rufus Marne's 'House of the Bears'. Dr. Palfrey is asked to journey there to examine an invalid - who has now disappeared. Moreover, Marne's daughter lies terribly injured after a fall from the minstrel's gallery which Dr. Palfrey discovers was no accident. He sets out to investigate and the results surprise even him . . . .

"'Palfrey' and his boys deserve to take their places among the immortals." - Western Mail

INTRODUCING THE TOFF

Whilst returning home from a cricket match at his father's country home, the Honourable Richard Rollison - alias The Toff - comes across an accident which proves to be a mystery. As he delves deeper into the matter with his usual perseverance and thoroughness , murder and suspense form the backdrop to a fast moving and exciting adventure.

'The Toff has been promoted to a place of honour among amateur detectives.' – The Times Literary Supplement